The Phantom Wolf of Lookout Mountain

Carl Watson

ISBN 979-8-88540-534-8 (paperback)
ISBN 979-8-88540-535-5 (digital)

Christian Faith Publishing
832 Park Avenue
Meadville, PA 16335
www.christianfaithpublishing.com

Printed in the United States of America

In honor of my grandson,
Tanner Allen Knight

CHAPTER 1

The Funeral

This was not the way to start a summer vacation.

Mike Watkins brushed back a wave of long, blonde hair and loosened his tie. Funerals were for grown-ups. Twelve-year-olds had no business at them. He gazed miserably out the back window of their SUV at the barren slopes forming the base of Lookout Mountain.

On the trail below, his parents and grandparents were slowly making their way to the Hollow Hills Cemetery. He could see the center of the graveyard where a long black hearse lingered next to a green awning.

Mike glanced at his cousin. "Come on, William. We might as well get moving." He opened the car door and pulled himself out of the back seat. Standing next to the door, he wiggled into his dress coat. In this part of New Mexico, folks don't dress up like they do in the city—funeral or not—but his folks weren't convinced. Though he was allowed to make many of his own decisions, this funeral was something they insisted he attend. He figured on taking as long as he could, especially since everyone moved out ahead, leaving no one to gripe at him.

"Hey!" yelled William, plowing into him from behind. "What're you doing? Trying to emulate a proverbial pillar of salt?"

"Em...pro...what?"

Mike turned and grabbed his stocky, round-faced relative by the front of his shirt. "Will, I don't care if you are my cousin. You're going to be pushing up a cactus right next to Joe if you don't stop acting like some college professor. Try talking like a real person."

William broke Mike's hold on him and shoved him back. "Take it easy, will you? You weren't the only one crammed in that back seat, you know." He frowned. "At least you're communicating, which is more than you've done since we left the ranch. Just 'cause you're annoyed having to be here, don't take it out on me. After all, it's no party for me either."

Mike's first inclination was to start an argument, but he thought a moment. There was no sense in disputing the truth. "Okay...so maybe you've got a point." He started moving toward the path leading down to the cemetery.

"Yeah, I figure Joe arranged it all," William said sarcastically, following close on Mike's heels. "He fell off that cliff just so we could arrive at the ranch in time for his funeral." William shoved his glasses up on his nose, pulled out his binoculars, and stopped to gaze at the mountain.

"That's not what I meant, and you know it," said Mike irritably as he slowly continued down the trail. "We barely knew him, so I don't think it's fair that we've gotta be here. That's all."

William said nothing.

Mike turned around, realizing William wasn't right behind him. He saw William standing on the side of the trail and moving his binoculars around to stare out across the prairie.

"Hey!" Mike shouted. "If I've gotta suffer through this, you're gonna have to suffer with me—without distractions." He glared at him. "Put that thing away."

William let out a long sigh. He shoved the binoculars back into the case strapped on his shoulder.

As Mike and William walked down the trail, a startled rabbit poked his head above a stand of prairie grass and ran off as if to warn others of the human invasion. The boys stopped behind the crowd near the canopy

Small, dark clouds created a host of creeping shadows that moved in ceaseless shifting patterns until they blended together in the distance. The mountain's peak appeared above the clouds and then hid again as if in respect of the event to come.

Mike stared uneasily at the coffin. Joe Sanchez had worked as Gramp's ranch foreman for many years. He was a silent man. Nobody knew him very well except the grand folks. Still, Mike couldn't forget Dad's warning. "If you two want to stay on your grandfather's good side, you'll be at the funeral, and you'll behave."

Again, Mike glanced up at Lookout Mountain. A cloudburst on the upper slopes hid the peaks behind a heavy, wet veil. Slowly, the clouds moved across a ridge in their direction. Perhaps a downpour would be a fitting way to end this graveside scene.

Mike was reminded of Uncle Charlie's funeral. It had ended with a thunderstorm. That happened about six years ago. Afterward, Uncle Charlie's son, William, came to live with them, his mother having died some years before. At first, Mike had resented William being there, but over time, he had learned to accept him as part of the family.

Suddenly, the preacher called for everyone's attention and began the service with a long prayer. Mike bowed his head. However, he didn't listen to the words. Instead, he thought about a question bothering him like a pesky fly buzzing inside his head.

Why would a guy who spent his life climbing around on a mountain suddenly fall off a cliff? He had asked his dad and got a lecture on mountain safety.

"All it takes is one moment of carelessness. Now understand, … and I'm serious. I don't want you guys up there. Is that clear?"

Mike had nodded, but at the same time, he felt that he and William were being lectured for somebody else's mistake. He knew the mountain—any mountain—could be dangerous if you didn't pay attention to what you were doing. The sheriff figured Joe had dismounted on a narrow ledge and lost his balance. That didn't make sense. What sane person would get off a horse in the middle of a narrow path high on the side of a mountain?

The preacher finished the prayer and started talking about what a great guy Joe had been. Mike's gaze returned to the people standing under the canopy. Other than his family, most of the people were his grandparent's friends from town and neighbors from nearby ranches. As he had figured, the great majority of them didn't wear coats and ties, but you'd never convince an eastern college professor like his father to change his ways.

One bearded mestizo stood alone outside the edge of the crowd. Stone faced, he stared at the preacher. He stood erect with a worn serape about his shoulders and a broad-brimmed hat pulled down over his straggly, white hair. He spoke to no one, his black eyes darting between the preacher and the casket.

Nudging William, Mike nodded toward the old man. "Look," he whispered. "Isn't that the shaman?"

"I think you're right," replied William. He added, "I certainly wouldn't want to be alone with such an ominous looking individual."

Those long words again. Mike whacked his cousin on the shoulder and stared at him as if he had turned into an alien.

A woman standing nearby frowned at them, and Mike looked back toward the preacher. After the woman's attention returned to the service, he poked William and whispered, "Save all those big words to impress the grownups. Now, talk American, will you?"

William shrugged. "All I meant was I wouldn't want to meet him by myself on a dark night."

"Well, why didn't you say that?" Mike shook his head. There were times he had trouble believing this smart aleck was related to him or his family. Still, he knew William didn't mean to sound like a stuck-up professor. He just hung out in a library too much.

The rest of the funeral didn't last very long. A light drizzle started, and a dull rumble came from behind the clouds above the mountain. The preacher gave a somber prayer. He led a gloomy hymn that everybody was supposed to know. Then someone placed a bouquet of drab-looking flowers on the casket before the preacher dismissed everybody with another prayer.

Without warning, the shaman stepped forward and raised one arm in the air. He looked toward the mountain and called out in a firm voice, "Beware, the Great White Wolf!"

Everyone stood in shocked silence as he turned and walked away, speaking to no one.

A chill traveled all the way down Mike's back to his toes. He whispered to William, "I wonder what kind of drugs that guy's on."

William pulled out his binoculars and shrugged indifferently. "At present, I lack sufficient information to…"

Mike kicked him in the shins.

"Ow!" William rubbed his leg. "I mean… I don't know."

The shaman left the cemetery, and the crowd dispersed. As the drizzle stopped, the clouds parted as if controlled by some supernatural force.

Mike glanced up the slope. "Will, zero in on that ledge. It looks like some kind of animal."

William swung his binoculars to the area where Mike pointed.

"Oh, wow. Awesome! Unbelievable!" Handing the binoculars to Mike, he added, "You may want to take back what you thought about the shaman."

Mike peered through the lenses and adjusted them to bring the object into focus. He gasped and readjusted them again as if the image might change.

A large, white wolf stood at the edge of a cliff, bathed in a single ray of sunlight.

CHAPTER 2

The Bunkhouse

After breakfast the next morning, Mike's father, Mr. Watkins, dug the bunkhouse key out of his pocket and handed it to Mike. "Your grandfather already got the most important stuff out of Joe's room. He needs help getting the rest."

"But, Dad, you said…" Mike pleaded.

"Mike," his father spoke firmly, "you and Will get that room cleaned out. Then, like I said, the rest of the day is yours."

Mike looped the string from the dangling key around his wrist. He sat at the kitchen table and fumed.

His mom stopped bustling about the kitchen and set the dishes in the sink. She brushed back the long, dark hair that had fallen over her eyes and put a hand on Mike's shoulder. "Your grandfather's counting on you."

Mike knew it wouldn't do any good to argue. If he tried, she would simply stare at him with her large, soft eyes. That would melt him on the spot and make him feel guilty for questioning her judgment. He let out a big sigh to let everybody know how he really felt, got up from the table, and motioned at his cousin. "C'mon, Will. Let's get with it."

Good ol' William. At times he would get his head set about doing something a certain way. Yet most of the time, he was pretty easygoing, and this was one job Mike didn't want to do alone.

Mike led the way to the back porch. He glanced across the meadow in time to see a pair of deer disappear into the trees beyond. The early morning sun cast long shadows through the valley, and Lookout Mountain reflected shades of green and brown against an azure sky. What a great day for fishing. He would much rather be sitting along the banks of a mountain stream trying to snag a tasty trout.

The bunkhouse stood about fifty yards at the back of the ranch house. A long, drab-looking building made of adobe, it had served as home for a dozen cowboys during the busy days of the early 1900s. Now, with only a small herd of cattle to care for, no one but the old foreman had been needed, and the old bunkhouse stood neglected with only a couple of rooms in livable condition. Other parts of the structure were used for storage.

Mike picked up a couple of empty boxes. "Grab some, Will."

"You sure this will be adequate?" asked William as he picked up another couple of boxes and balanced one on his head.

"I don't know if they're adequate or not," Mike answered dryly, "but if they're not enough, we'll come back and get some more."

He started across the yard. About halfway, he stopped and stared at the old, gray building. It looked changed somehow—colorless and sad, like it had died right along with old Joe. "Will, you notice anything different about the bunkhouse?" he asked uneasily. His eyes glued on the building.

"No, not really," said William while taking a picture of the building with his iPhone. He studied the picture for a moment, returned the phone to his shirt pocket, and stooped over to pick up a box he had dropped.

"It…it looks strange. It's kind of stiff and still…like a tombstone." Mike shook his head, trying to make the image merge into something different.

William set the box down and pulled out his phone again. "That excursion to the cemetery yesterday really got to you, didn't it?"

Watching him trying to focus the phone again on the entire length of the bunkhouse, Mike chuckled. "It certainly didn't affect you. You still look like a tourist."

"Our teacher suggested we keep a record of everything we do this summer," said William. He shoved his glasses back up on his nose and stepped back to snap a picture of Mike with the bunkhouse in the background. "What better kind of record is there other than a pictorial one?"

Mike frowned. Who, other than William, would ever use such a word as "pictorial"?

"Yeah," he said. "Pictures are great." He shook his head and continued walking toward the front of the building. There were times he wondered if William had been adopted from another planet. Only, everybody must be keeping it a secret. He scrambled up the bunkhouse steps and continued toward the door. The porch complained noisily as he tromped across it.

William stood at the bottom step and rubbed his chin. "I really don't believe in apparitions, but I hear spirits will sometimes return to places they know best."

"About all we need now is for that wolf to show up," muttered Mike. "That would make the scene complete." He studied the bunkhouse windows as if he expected to see a ghostly figure watching them.

"How did we get stuck with doing this anyway?" said William with a shudder.

"Cause Dad told us to, that's why." Mike set down the boxes and fumbled with the key. He added, "You know, that wolf showing up when he did might just have been a co...co..."

"Coincidence," said William in a matter-of-fact manner.

"Yeah, and it was sure weird."

A creaking sound came from one end of the porch.

"What's that?" Mike took a step backward and froze as he watched an old rocking chair move slowly back and forth in the breeze. He whispered in a shaky voice, "There's another co-co-coincidence."

"At least it's not a wolf," William said, staring at it with widened eyes.

Mike decided he was letting his imagination get the best of him. Talking to himself as much as to William, he whispered, "It's only the wind." He swallowed hard, turned his back toward the rocking chair, and grunted as he jiggled the key in the lock.

It wouldn't turn.

"We're the only ones here," he said loudly. "Only reason this place seems so weird is 'cause it's old." He didn't really know the age of the bunkhouse, but the words sounded good.

"Yeah, that's probably an accurate analysis of the situation," said William, talking a bit fast and breathing heavily. He climbed the steps behind Mike.

Mike ignored him and peered at the windows. They glared back at him with a dead, empty stare. "As I was saying, we're just here to box up Joe's stuff," he said, his voice a few decibels higher than normal.

"Then we'll be gone," added William with a panicky edge to his voice.

Finally, with another jiggle and a loud grunt, Mike turned the key and shoved the door open. He picked up the boxes and peered inside. Hesitantly, he stepped inside with William close behind. The well-worn floor creaked with each step as he and Will made their way down the gloomy hall. Mike stopped at the door to Joe's room.

"Well, here we are," said William. His attempt at enthusiasm sounded fake and hollow.

A rustling sound came from somewhere ahead, and Mike stared toward the dark end of the hall. "What's that?" he asked in a forced whisper. To answer his own question, he added, "Bet the rats have a party every day without a lot of people around."

William swayed from one foot to the other as if he were having trouble deciding whether to stay or to make a dash for the door. As Mike balanced his boxes with one hand and reached for a doorknob, William poked him.

Mike jumped. "You idiot! What'd you do that for?"

Whispering, William asked, "Are you certain Joe would approve of us being here? He never once invited us to his room when he was alive."

"I… I know." Mike turned the knob and slowly pushed open the door. He gasped, "Oh wow."

The room looked as if a giant hand had picked it up and shook it. Drawers lay about and heaps of clothes were strewed across the room. Scattered pieces of the bed frame appeared in various places. Even the bedsprings leaned against the wall as if resting from battle. A table and a broken lamp lay on their sides next to a pair of throw rugs.

"Zeesh." William's mouth dropped open. "I knew some bachelors were disorganized, but this is ridiculous."

"Dad said Granddad had already been here, but he wouldn't leave it like this." Mike dropped the boxes and tried the light switch, but nothing happened.

"I don't think Joe would have left it like this either." William set his boxes on a mattress and pulled back the curtains.

"Will, I don't like it. Somebody's been looking for something."

"That's obvious." William wandered about, pushing clothes and books around with his foot. "But for what?" He pulled out his phone and moved to a corner of the room where he turned and snapped a picture.

The flash from William's phone startled Mike so badly he almost fell over the boxes. "Will," he shouted, rubbing his eyes, "what the heck are you doing?"

"Getting a picture."

"Why?"

"Because that's what any good investigator does."

"Who said we're investigators?"

"We want to find out who did this and why, don't we?"

"Well, yeah. I guess so."

"Well," announced William jubilantly, "that makes us investigators." He studied the picture he had taken.

"Whatever." Mike shrugged. He glanced around the room. "I don't understand. Why would anyone mess up Joe's stuff like this? He didn't have anything actually worth much. He was just a ranch foreman. All he had was a beat-up saddle and a horse."

"Maybe he took a picture of a drug buy or a murder," said William mysteriously. "Maybe somebody wants to locate his phone before the criminal goes to trial and it's brought out as evidence. Maybe that's why he had an accident."

"You've been watching too much TV again." Mike snickered. "This isn't the city. We're on a ranch, remember?"

"So? What explanation do you have?"

"I don't have one yet." Mike scratched his head.

"Maybe they found it," William pulled out his shirttail and wiped his glasses with it.

"Found what?"

"Whatever they were doing all this heavy looking for."

"Shh," Mike said suddenly. He heard a movement in the hallway that made him freeze to the spot, his heart pounding.

William stopped and stood stock-still. He put his glasses back on and whispered, "Let's go. Now."

Mike motioned at him to stay put. "There's only this one door, remember?"

He grabbed an old shoe from under a bunk and, standing next to the door, he raised it, ready to clobber the first thing that appeared.

CHAPTER 3

The Stable

Mike held his breath. Slowly, he let it out and inhaled again. He listened as hard as he could, but he couldn't hear another sound. Sweat trickled down his back, and his arm got tired. Maybe the whole thing was his imagination working overtime. William stood behind him as stiff as the wall he was leaning against.

Suddenly, a small, gray shadow shot across his foot followed by a larger streak of black.

William shrieked like he was being attacked and dove for the mattress.

"Murky!" exclaimed Mike, "You stupid cat." He dropped the shoe and exhaled a big breath of air.

Murky meowed a greeting. With a swish of her tail, she stared at a hole near the base of a wall where the gray shadow had disappeared.

William shoved his glasses up on his nose, rolled off the mattress, and picked her up. He patted her rounded stomach and chuckled. "I think she and I have something in common. We're both avoiding starvation."

"Yeah, but it still looks like she's been able to keep everybody on their toes," said Mike, peering at the small hole in the baseboard. He marveled at how the mouse had been able to squeeze through it so quickly.

"Well, at least, most everybody," added William, gazing thoughtfully around the messy room.

"You know, there's something weird about this whole business; the shaman, the white wolf, and now this room." Mike glanced at William. "What do you make of it?"

"I'm not sure." William set Murky down, grabbed an armload of Joe's clothes, and packed them into a box. "What would someone want from Joe important enough to trash his room? And what does this shaman and the wolf have to do with…with anything?"

Mike walked across the room and picked up a shirt.

"Mike!" shrieked William.

"What?" Mike's heart skipped a beat, and he dropped the shirt as if it had suddenly come to life.

"Look at this." William held up a photograph he had found on a table, his eyes wide with excitement.

Mike shot across the room and snatched it out of William's hand. He raised an eyebrow. It was a photo of Joe and his horse. "So?"

"If Joe hid something he didn't want anybody to have, but that somebody wants and nobody's found, I bet I know where somebody hasn't looked."

"You've lost it, Will." Exasperated, Mike stared at him. "For somebody who's so good with words, you've jumbled them up like shuffled dominoes. What're you talking about?"

"The saddlebags!" William pointed at the photo. "He spent more time on that horse than anywhere."

They both glanced out the window at the stable.

"C'mon." Mike grabbed William's arm and tugged him toward the door.

"But…but," spluttered William, "what about all this paraphernalia?"

Mike hesitated a moment and stared at him. "If you mean all his stuff, we'll get to that later."

***

13

A lifeless-looking structure, the stable had stalls for twenty horses. Now only four were occupied. Some contained feed for the animals. Others were empty, their scarred railings standing as reminders of a much busier time.

Mike found an old saddlebag lying across a railing. He slapped one of the pockets.

"This has got to be it," he said gleefully. He lifted one of the flaps and felt inside.

"Well?" William asked impatiently.

"This is his saddlebag all right." Mike pulled out a harmonica, a tattered old notebook, and a stubby pencil. "Remember when he was talking about how music keeps the cattle calm on a stormy night?"

William ducked under the railing to the other side and lifted the other flap. He reached inside the pocket and groped around. "Nothing. Well, so much for that bright idea."

Mike picked up the notebook. As he flipped through it, a piece of paper fell out. He unfolded it and spread it on the ground. "Hey, Will, this is a page from a book, a history book I think."

"So?"

"So what's Joe doing with it?"

"Look, some of the words are circled," said William, staring at it over Mike's shoulder.

"I can see that," Mike snapped. "But listen to this.

> On April 20, 1881, the Albuquerque City Bank reported a robbery of several thousand dollars, most of which were in gold coin. The money had been placed in a railroad car destined for Denver. At about 3:00 p.m., the train was boarded by a group of ruffians between Raton and Santa Fe near the small town of Springer. The robbers were alleged to be members of the Deaton Gang wearing false beards and dusters, a well-known trademark of this notorious group."

"Wow!"

Mike studied the picture of a bearded man on horseback wearing a long coat and wondered how they could stand them in the heat of summer.

"Look, here's something else." William pointed at another circled paragraph.

Mike held the paper closer to the light. It said: "A guard on the railcar identified one of the robbers as Sam Deaton, the leader of the group. He overheard Sam instructing his men to meet at The Spaniard if separated."

"Look at how 'The Spaniard' was underlined," William added, looking over Mike's shoulder.

"Yeah," said Mike, with a strong tinge of curiosity in his voice. "I wonder what 'The Spaniard' is."

"It goes on to say that authorities looked in every town within a hundred miles," continued William. He took the paper from Mike and gazed at it. "Nobody ever found a saloon or anything else called The Spaniard. They chased down a couple of the robbers and killed them in a gun battle, but the gold and the rest of the gang were never seen again."

William handed the paper back to Mike and climbed up on a railing. "Maybe Joe found 'The Spaniard,' and that's why his room was trashed. Some unscrupulous fortune hunter was looking for information."

Mike added, "I'd bet that 'un-scoop-a-las' fortune hunter isn't a very nice guy either." He stared blankly at the paper for a moment. Joe's death involved more than just a careless step off the edge of a cliff. He was certain of it.

Turning to William, he said in a nervous whisper, "I think we're getting to the real reason for Joe's so-called accident."

"Let me see that again." Grabbing the paper, William dropped off the railing and moved into the sunlight near the doorway. "Hey, this page is not from any ordinary schoolbook." Shoving his glasses farther up on his nose, he pointed to the heading. "It's from Unsolved Crimes of the Nineteenth Century, and here it talks about a map on the next page." He scratched his head and bent over to stare more closely at the paper. "This is a xeroxed copy and not a very good one at that. Look how out-of-focus the letters are along this inside edge. I wonder where Joe got it."

Mike frowned. "Dummy, you of all people ought to know that."

"Oh?"

"Why, a library, of course, and the nearest one's in Springer."

"Awesome!" William grinned from ear to ear. "I want to see that map. Let's get somebody to take us there."

"C'mon." Mike took off for the house with William close on his heels.

CHAPTER 4

The Library

Finding a ride into Springer was not a problem. Mike's mother planned to get a few things from the store, so Mike asked her to let them off at the library.

"You want to go where?" She brushed the hair back out of her eyes and gave him a strange look.

"The library," he repeated with a sheepish grin.

"Now let me get this straight. All year, you two talked about coming out here to the ranch where you can fish, ride horses, and explore. Now you want to go to a library?" She felt his head. "Are you feeling all right? You don't seem to have a fever."

"Aw, Mom." Mike shoved her hand away and sighed. "Don't make such a big deal about it. We just want to look up some stuff about the history of this place."

William nodded.

"If that's what you want, hop in." Mike's mother shrugged. She walked around to the driver's side of the old station wagon muttering, "Kids sure have changed since I was little."

Mike clutched the piece of paper they found and stared out the back window all the way to Springer. He puzzled over the strange events they had experienced since the day they arrived at the funeral. Was there really a connection between a robbery from over a century ago and the death of Joe? Where did the shaman and the white wolf fit into the picture?

"I should be back in about thirty minutes," said Mike's mother as she let them out in front of the library. "Call me on my cell if I'm not here by then."

Mike checked his phone to make sure it was on. "That should be plenty of time," he said. With a wave of the hand, he added, "We'll meet you out here."

***

Mike knew Roscoe Sweeney. He managed the local theater on weekends, selling popcorn and running the projector. During the week, he supervised the public library. Each morning, he would slide himself in place behind the front desk with a magazine and soda.

Roscoe stared at Mike and William above the frames of his thick-rimmed glasses. His greeting always consisted of a snickering laugh that made Mike cringe. It seemed to say he knew you were guilty of something, but he'd keep it a secret.

"Heh heh heh. Well, well…haven't seen the two of you in a month of Sundays. In fact, it's a first for here, isn't it? How're things going?"

"Fine," said Mike with a nod.

Roscoe laughed again, scratched his nose, and peered at them. "Heard about ol' Joe. That's a real shame. But, you know, that mountain can be dangerous." He dropped his head and stared at them over his glasses again. "I reckon things are pretty quiet out at the ranch."

"Everything's fine," said William. He changed the subject. "We're searching for a historical publication about robbers."

Mike poked William and frowned. Nobody needed to know why they were there, and certainly not Roscoe, the biggest gossip in town.

The librarian's eyes narrowed into slits. He chuckled. "Haven't decided to take up a life of crime, have you?"

"Course not," piped up Mike. Abruptly, he changed the subject. "What's showing at the movies this weekend?"

Roscoe's face eased into a cheesy smile making Mike think of the painted Mardi Gras masks on the wall of an art gallery. "We got a good oldie called *The Mummy Lives*." He glanced at William. "Any certain book I can help you find?"

"Naw," interrupted Mike, "we're just…just looking. Come on, Will."

Roscoe chuckled again. He called after them. "If there's anything I can do for you boys, just let me know."

When they got out of earshot, Mike grabbed William's arm. He whispered, "Dummy, we can't let him know what we're after. When gold's involved, you can't trust anyone."

"I don't see what you're so bent out of shape about," said William jerking his arm away. "I just told him we were interested in a bit of history."

"I know. You told him we were"—Mike tilted back his head with his nose in the air—"interested in a historical publication about robbers."

William chuckled. "So? What's wrong with that?"

"Maybe nothing. I just know you can't be too careful."

At the computer, Mike searched in the listings under Titles. "Hey, it's here."

Mike kept the index number in his head as he and William trotted to the shelves. They started at opposite ends and walked toward the middle.

"I found it." Mike pulled *Unsolved Crimes of the Nineteenth Century* from a shelf. William joined him. They sat on the floor and turned to the page that had been xeroxed. The next page was supposed to contain a map, but it was missing.

"This is a waste of time," muttered William.

"No, it's not," argued Mike. "It proves the map was important. Else why would somebody rip it out?"

"Hmm, a good assumption," said William thoughtfully. "But it doesn't solve anything."

"Yeah, but it means we could be on to something. I mean, who'd do something like this unless there's a mighty good reason?"

"Maybe Joe had a reason." William's lips tightened. "Then again, somebody else could have ripped it out later."

Mike gazed out the window. What William suggested made the most sense. If Joe tore out the map, he would have taken out the other page across from it as well instead of just xeroxing it. How important was that map? Did Joe see a clue on the map showing where the robbers put the gold? Did somebody kill him to get it? Maybe he made a copy of it and hid it somewhere. But where?

William moved to a window and pulled out the photo he took at the bunkhouse. "The light in this place is sure lacking, especially for a library," he muttered.

A tingle went up Mike's spine.

"Will! The light!"

"I know. That's what I just said."

Mike grabbed him by the shoulder. "No, no, you dodo. The light...not here...the picture!" His words jumped about trying to catch up with his thoughts, making it hard to get them out. He held out his hand. "Here, let me see that."

William handed him the photo.

"Look." Mike pointed at the top of it. "The light fixture on the ceiling—it's got a shade."

"So?"

"The light didn't work. Remember, I tried the switch."

"So?" William stirred impatiently.

"Wouldn't that be a good place to hide a piece of paper—like a map?"

The boys stared at each other for a moment.

William exclaimed, "Let's go!"

Mike grabbed the book as he headed down the aisle to the front. "We'll check this out. There might be something in it we haven't found."

At the checkout desk, Roscoe didn't seem to be in any hurry. "You're getting this one?" he asked.

"Yeah," said Mike casually. "I thought we might find some interesting stuff in it."

Roscoe laughed in his weird, snickering way. "You might find some good instructions on how to rob banks in it."

"I don't think we're interested in that particular activity," said William. "We'll relinquish that brand of malevolence to the computer wizards of modern day. Anyway, this publication would be a little archaic for assisting with such a contemporary feat as that, don't you think?"

Silence.

Roscoe laughed nervously and shoved his glasses up on his nose. "You...you got a point, I think." He stamped the due date on the card. "See you at the movies."

"Yes, sir. Bye." William snatched up the book and left.

Mike shut the door behind them and burst out laughing.

"What's so amusing?" William shrugged innocently.

"'Brand of malev...whatever you said." Mike laughed and whacked William on the shoulder. He pulled out his cell phone.

"Grown-ups are so easily impressed," said William with a chuckle. "That's my newest word and I had been looking for a chance to use it."

"Some people are a lot more out of it than others," said Mike, gesturing back toward the door with his head. He punched a button on his phone.

In a moment, his mother answered, telling him she was on the way.

As they waited, Mike sat on the curb while William studied the book.

"The Spaniard?" muttered William. He scratched his head. "Could that be a painting in an art museum?"

"I thought about that," said Mike. "But back then, I don't believe there were any museums—least not around here."

William snapped his fingers. "I know. We'll ask Granddad. He's lived in this area all his life."

"Good idea," Mike said brightly. He jumped to his feet as the station wagon pulled up to the curb. "Here's Mom."

"I see you found something," said Mike's mother as they piled into the back seat.

21

"Yeah…something," said Mike.

William added, "But not everything."

Mrs. Dunlap turned and looked at them. "Huh?"

"Don't mind him," said Mike as he poked his cousin. "He's just trying to be funny."

"Oh." His mother brushed back her hair, switched on the radio, and they started for home.

CHAPTER 5

The Map

As his mother drove back to the ranch, Mike studied the photograph while William reread the page about the train robbery.

Mike wasn't sure, but there could be a shadow inside the shade of the light fixture. What if Joe was trying to find the gold coins and took a copy of the map to help him figure out where they were? What if somebody else knew about the coins and didn't like the competition? Joe's death was no accident. He felt sure of it.

"Are you two finished boxing everything in Joe's room yet?"

Mike looked at his mom's face in the rearview mirror. He shook his head. "I figure we'll do that when we get back."

She smiled back at him. "I know your grandfather appreciates your help. If somebody comes to claim Joe's things, it'll be nice to have them ready."

"I was wondering," said Mike. "Did Granddad find anything interesting when he looked through Joe's stuff?"

"Not much." His mother knitted her dark eyebrows into a frown. "We hoped to find something about Joe's relatives. In fact, the sheriff's still trying to help us locate someone."

The station wagon pulled up in the drive, and the boys piled out. They dashed for the bunkhouse. The unlocked door swung open, and they stumbled through it like a pair of clowns in a circus act.

"I knew Granddad wouldn't have left such a mess," said Mike. He tugged a table under the light fixture in Joe's room. "Someone came along after him."

"Yeah, but who?" William put a chair on top of the table and held the legs while Mike climbed on it.

"Maybe Joe had a few so-called friends no one knew about," said Mike.

"Some friends," William muttered.

Mike ran his hand around the inside of the shade and pulled out a piece of paper.

"Bingo!" he shouted. Hopping down, he spread the paper out on the floor. "This is it." He traced a doubled line across the paper with his finger. "These are the railroad tracks between Santa Fe and Raton."

William looked over his shoulder and pointed. "There's an X near Springer which is probably where the holdup happened."

"Yeah, but what's all this other stuff? It looks like there's a creek of some kind and a couple of hand-drawn X's. One of them has the word *cave* near it, and the other has *con...con...*"

"Conquistador!" announced William.

"Hey, that's a...a soldier of some kind?"

"Yeah. The Spaniard!" William's eyes grew large, and he grinned from ear to ear. "It's a Spanish soldier."

"Could be." Mike glanced up at William and raised an eyebrow thoughtfully. "Here folks have been looking for a bar or a painting when maybe it's a statue...or a rock formation." He gazed back at the map. "And isn't that Lookout Mountain? Wow, that means it's here—somewhere near the west corner of our north pasture."

"Let's go!" William hopped to his feet.

"It looks kind of far," said Mike. "Maybe we'd better see if we can get a couple of horses and go out in the morning."

"Granddad!" William exclaimed. "Remember, we need to talk with him anyway. Let's ask."

***

Granddad was using a hoe to weed the flowers along the side of the house. He wore a pair of overalls and an old slouch hat that made him look more like a Texas farmer than a rancher in New Mexico.

Mike knew better than to just flat out tell his grandfather what they wanted. He knew that with him, you had to go easily, one step at a time. He strolled up behind him.

"Hi, Granddad. What are you doing?"

Granddad stopped hoeing and gazed at him from under his heavy, white eyebrows. "Guess."

"Your flowers are sure neat," said William. "Delphiniums, aren't they?"

"How'd you know?"

"You raised them here last year." William cupped one in his hand and took a closer look. "You told us all about them."

Granddad leaned on his hoe and scratched his mustache. "Didn't think you'd remember."

"They take a lot of care, don't they?" said William.

His grandfather grinned. "Actually, they don't need much help. However, they don't mind you getting rid of a few of their weedy companions every now and then."

Mike sat on the ground, Indian style. "We need to ask a question," he said.

"Ask."

"Was there anything strange about Joe's room when you went there to find out stuff about his relatives?"

Granddad shook his head. "No, 'cept I never found anything."

"He sure had an untidy room, didn't he?" asked William.

"Not really. Why?"

"It was messy when we got to it," said Mike. "I can't tell anything's missing, but it looks like someone's been there, digging through stuff."

Granddad frowned and tugged at his mustache, which Mike knew to be a sign of solemn thought. "Boys, I need you to check all the windows and make sure everything's locked up tight. Especially now that no one's staying there, it's an open invitation for hobos and tramps."

"Yes, sir," Mike answered. "We'll take care of it." He bit on his lower lip and asked, "By the way, is there anything interesting in the north pasture?"

"Or unusual," added William as he flopped down next to Mike. "Why?"

"Thought we might take Big Red and Cimarron up there to look around a bit," said Mike.

"There're some interesting bits of history in the hills up there above the pasture. Every now and then, somebody finds names or dates scratched in the rocks. There're even some Indian writings up there...in a cave."

Mike and William grinned at each other.

Granddad lifted an eyebrow. "The horses haven't had much exercise in the past couple of weeks. Might be good to let 'em stretch their legs a bit." He looked at Mike and added, "If your father agrees. Remember, a cell phone won't work up there in the valley."

"We won't need one," said William.

"Thanks, Granddad," said Mike. He rolled over and backflipped to his feet. Punching William on the shoulder, he added, "We've got to finish those boxes. Race you."

William scrambled up and away they went.

They returned to Joe's room, packed the boxes, cleaned the room, and straightened it. William checked the windows to make sure they were locked.

Mike had just stacked the last box in the corner of the room when he thought of something and froze. "Hey."

"Hey, what?"

Mike pulled the paper from his pocket and smoothed it out on a table. "Something else."

"What's that?"

"Look at this map...the smudgy sides of it."

"So?"

"This is another xeroxed copy."

William shrugged. "So?"

"So who's got the original? It's not in the book."

"Oh, wow."

They stared at each other.

Mike gulped. "Just think. Whoever's got it just might be the somebody that killed Joe."

CHAPTER 6

The Spaniard

"Hey, wait up!"

Mike reined in Big Red to wait for William to catch up. The horse snorted and shook its head, so Mike patted his neck and bent over to talk into his ear.

"Now look," he warned. "Let's you and I get to an understanding. I didn't have to take you on this trip, you know. I could have left you standing in the stable to be bored all day. So behave yourself and don't give me any trouble, or that's where you'll end up for the rest of the summer. Okay?"

Again, Big Red snorted.

Mike added, "And no back talk, understand?"

He turned in the saddle and called to William, "Hey, what's holding you up?"

"I'm getting there," called William. He grabbed the reins as his horse stopped to nibble on a bush. "Cimarron is enjoying himself—perhaps a little too much."

"Big Red and I just had a little man to horse talk."

William snickered. "What man?"

"The only man out here, of course." Mike sat up straight and threw his shoulders back.

"I don't see any hair on your chest."

Mike unbuttoned his shirt and peered beneath it. He shrugged. "Hey, I'm working on it." Nodding toward the north, he added, "Let's follow that gully."

"Lead on, O mighty warrior," exclaimed William dramatically with a touch of sarcasm.

Mike hadn't been on a horse since last summer, but as Granddad had said, "Once a horseman, always a horseman"—or something like that. Leading toward the gully across a broad meadow, he drew in a deep breath. The air smelled clean and felt crisp following a shower from the night before, and the warmth of the sun felt good on his back.

His dad had given his standard lecture that morning. They were to stay together, not race the horses and walk them if they got tired, stop at the stream for water, and so on and so on. Mike pretty well had it all memorized.

He nudged Big Red with his knees. A winding trail followed the gully away before threading between a pair of boulders and dropping into a shallow valley.

Turning to William, he nodded ahead. "There's the creek we saw on the map."

"Looking good," said William.

They dismounted, watered the horses, and started climbing while pulling the animals behind them. The trail passed through a draw and dropped into a narrow canyon with high, steep walls. At the north end, a crumbled mass of rocks and boulders filled the space between the canyon walls. Mike stopped to stare as William trudged up behind him.

"I wonder when that happened," said Mike.

"Glad I wasn't here when it did," said William, scratching his head.

They tied their horses to a bush, and Mike climbed the first boulder. He called back. "Will, there's a penlight in my saddlebag. Bring it with you, okay?"

"Of course," William grumbled. "How about a pillow as well—in case you fall on your butt?"

"Very funny," said Mike, making a face. "But think about it. Wouldn't this be a good place to stash a bag of gold?"

"All right, all right," snapped William. "I'll get your light. However, I'm of the opinion that…"

"Will," shouted Mike. "Get on with it, will you?"

"Okay, I'm coming."

Mike looked at places where huge boulders had rolled against each other. Any of the spaces created would be more than large enough to hide stolen bags of coins. Of course, they could also be a home for snakes, spiders, or who knows what.

"Hurry up!" he bellowed as he hopped from the top of one boulder to another. Between two of the rocks, a space existed seeming larger than the others. He walked to the edge of it and peered down. Enough light seeped through he could see the ground below.

Mike turned to holler at William again, but before he could utter a sound, he felt part of the rock crumble beneath his feet. Too late, he tried to jump. Instead, he tumbled with a shower of pebbles to the clearing inside.

William appeared overhead.

"Mike!" he yelled. "You all right?"

"Yeah," gasped Mike. He took a deep breath. "I just got a bit—of wind—knocked out of me. Drop me the light."

William did so, and Mike flashed it on the walls around him. He could see there were plenty of crevices and niches.

"Getting out won't be a problem," he shouted. He studied a set of lines etched into the side of a boulder. At first, he thought it resembled some sort of man-made foothold. Then he looked a second time, and his heart skipped a beat.

"Will," he yelled.

"What?"

"I found it!"

"You found what?"

"The…the Spaniard."

Mike caught his breath. There could be no doubt—the high collar, the trimmed beard, the hat. Someone from long ago had carved the outline of a Spanish soldier from the early 18th century into the face of a stone. They had scratched the date 1722 below the figure.

"What?"

"Get down here." Mike flashed his light up along the wall. "You'd never believe it. It's here…right here. Just drop your feet over the side. There're plenty of places along the rock to climb down."

He urged, "C'mon, you've got to see this."

In a moment, William had dropped to the floor of the cave-like area. He stared at the ancient drawing and whistled.

"Awesome. A conquistador! Who'd ever believe…?"

"And look at this," interrupted Mike. He pointed at the initials *S.D.* marked on the Spaniard's forehead.

"That's just what some idiot left so he could brag he'd been here," said William with a sigh.

"Oh, yeah?" Mike stared. That familiar tingle was attacking his spine again. He pulled the information sheet from his back pocket and spread it on the ground. "That's him!"

"What?"

"Not what. Who. It's Sam Deaton."

"You mean Sam Deaton was a Spaniard?" said William, looking puzzled.

"You idiot, I'm talking about the initials." Mike folded the paper and jammed it back in his pocket. "S.D. for Sam Deaton, the leader of the gang."

"Oh wow." William took Mike's light and reexamined the face on the rock. "The rock slid! That explains why nobody located him." He stepped back to look at the entire drawing. "There's even a small arrow here. I don't understand though. Why would this Deaton guy leave his initials?"

"Remember, they were all supposed to meet here at the Spaniard," said Mike punctuating his words with dramatic gestures, "but the article in that book said a couple of them got killed in a gun battle. Sam Deaton didn't know that. He must have left the arrow and his initials to show them they should keep going on up the canyon."

"To where?" asked William.

"To wherever all that gold is they had to have been lugging around," exclaimed Mike. "We need to be moving!"

Without hesitation, Mike scaled the wall of the pit and helped William out behind him. They climbed on over to the back of the boulders where the trail reappeared. It continued upward along one side of the canyon wall.

"Let's keep track of the time," said Mike. He checked his watch as he started climbing the trail. "If we don't get home before supper, Dad will come looking for us."

"It's plenty early," said William.

"Oh yeah. Where've I heard that before? Last year when we were late getting home once, he grounded us for a whole week, and I don't think I could handle that—not with a whole bag of gold up here somewhere just waiting for us."

"All right," agreed William. "You made your point." He tripped over a rock and grabbed another to keep from rolling down the slope back into the canyon.

"You also had better watch where you're going." Mike reached down, grabbed William's wrist, and helped him back up on the trail.

"You know, I wasn't really sure before." William coughed and took a deep breath. "But now I'm about convinced. That treasure's up there."

Mike nodded. "Yeah, just think. Those robbers must've come this way almost a hundred years ago lugging all that gold along with them."

"I bet they stopped to rest every now and then." William pulled up his shirttail and wiped the sweat off his face.

"I wonder how far they got." Mike glanced up. The trail passed out of the canyon and meandered up onto a slope containing a field of boulders. After twisting and winding through the rocks, it disappeared near the base of a solid, smooth wall.

"What's going on?" Mike stared and scratched his head.

"That trail has got to go somewhere," argued William.

"Yeah," agreed Mike. He grinned. "It seems like I remember this happening to somebody else once." He took a step backward and planted himself in the middle of the trail. Raising his arms toward the wall, he shouted, "I command you. Open Sesame!"

Nothing happened.

CHAPTER 7

Abandoned

William chuckled. "You're nuts."

He walked along the base of the cliff until he came to a gnarly, old pine growing up against the face of the rock. There, he found a foothold and started scaling it.

Mike laughed. "Hey, let me know if you start to fall," he teased. "I'll move out of the way."

William looked like a miniature grizzly clawing his way up the side of a mountain. Reaching a lower branch of the tree, he paused and puffed a moment.

"All right," he shouted. He peered down at Mike and added between breaths. "I think...this will get us...where we want to go."

"Are you sure?" asked Mike, gazing up at William's backside hanging over the trunk. Again, he laughed. "Looks like a dead end to me."

Ignoring the comment, William gave out a long, low whistle. "Awesome!"

"There you go with that *awesome* stuff again," said Mike. "What is it this time?"

"Come on up. This is something you've got to see for yourself."

Mike climbed up the tree. He grabbed the back of William's belt, pulled himself up to where he could see across the top of a narrow ledge that sealed off one end of a small valley. There, a clear stream flowed through the center of a green meadow.

"Hey, looks like a good place to explore," he exclaimed.

The two of them climbed out on a limb and dropped from the tree to the top of the ledge. They clambered down the rocks on the west side into the meadow. Struggling through waist-high grass, they worked their way to the stream. Water spurted out of the mountain partway up the cliff, creating a silvery waterfall.

"Awesome," repeated William.

"Yeah, and—oh, wow!" Mike pointed to the slopes north of the falls where a cave opened out on the rise above them.

"That must be what Granddad was talking about." William squinted. "You can see the hieroglyphics all the way from here."

Mike started to make another crack about William's vocabulary. Instead, he sighed and decided to give it up as a lost cause. "Come on, let's take a look."

The boys scrambled up the slope. Mike studied markings on the rock near the cave's entrance, and William traced them with his finger.

One drawing consisted of a group of crudely drawn animals that were probably wolves. They were sitting behind a large circle of flames watching a tribe of Indians dancing. Mike thought about that. He would have expected to see Indians watching the animals instead of the other way around.

"It must be a ceremony of some kind," he said scratching his head.

William took Mike's light and moved farther into the cave. "This might be an ideal location to conceal a bag of gold."

"I don't know about that," said Mike in a matter-of-fact tone. "It seems if something like that were hidden in here, it would have been found a long time ago."

"Hey," said William. "Here's something else awesome. Come here."

"Why?" Mike frowned. To him, the idea of stumbling around in a cave with one small light seemed akin to trying to pin a tail on a donkey while blindfolded. "It's time to head home. We can get a lantern and come back tomorrow."

"Aw, come on," urged William. "The cave is shallow. You can see this."

Mike sighed but plodded into the cave. The depth of the wide-mouthed cavern only extended a few feet from the entrance. This allowed enough light for them to wander without stumbling on the uneven ground, but the drawings on the wall were hard to see.

"Look." William flashed his light across one of the drawings. "These markings are different from the others. They're bigger and carved into the wall."

"Here, let me see." That all-familiar tingle moved up Mike's spine again. He grabbed the light and studied the drawing one part at a time.

"Great land of Goshen!" He stared intently at the lines etched into the surface of the rock. "Indians wouldn't draw anything like this. It's the map. See, here are the railroad tracks and Sombrero Peak. There's a C with a circle around it."

"Awesome." William stood on his tiptoes to see over Mike's shoulder. "Do you reckon that means a cave…this cave?"

Ignoring the question, Mike traced the marking with his finger. "Here's another arrow. It points to a line…like a trail moving up the mountain." He pulled the map out of his pocket and with a stubby pencil, copied the additions.

"But here's this circle again." William reached around him to feel the markings. "It looks like flames with groups of little animals around it. And here's another C."

"Hmm," said Mike. "Must be another cave. Look at the big X."

William grabbed Mike's arm. "That's where the gold is!" He almost jumped up and down with excitement. Grabbing a gulp of air, he continued, "That Deaton guy had it all planned out. He waited here with his gang. When the ones that were killed didn't appear, he created this map and left." He started for the cave's entrance. "C'mon. What're we waiting for?"

Outside, they searched the area behind the entrance. They found a faint trail continuing up the side of Lookout Mountain, and William started to climb.

"Wait a minute." Mike folded the map and stuck it in his pocket. He motioned toward the sun that appeared to be resting on the mountain's summit before dropping behind it. "It's getting late. Let's come back tomorrow."

"What?" William stopped and stared at him in amazement. "You're standing there, worried about the time of day when we are about to make the discovery of this century?"

"You don't know that, and soon it will be dark." Stubbornly, Mike stood his ground. He couldn't believe William had gotten gold fever so quickly. "That trail may lead nowhere. Dad will be here looking for us if we mess around much longer. If he finds us here, we'll not only be grounded for a week; we'll be grounded for the rest of the summer. Remember, he flat out told us he didn't want us on Lookout Mountain."

"When did he say that?"

"Just before the funeral."

"I didn't hear him."

"You were asleep."

"Really?" William laughed. "I think you're just scared of wolves or apparitions or something."

Mike felt the blood rush to his head. "Are you calling me a coward?"

"You said it. I didn't."

"Now look, stupid," said Mike. "Think about it a minute. We've got all the time in the world to explore this trail. It's not worth getting in trouble for when we can come back later and spend a whole day."

"You look." William pointed at him. "That's just a cop-out. First of all, we won't be that late."

"You bet your bottom we won't. Least ways I won't." Mike turned back toward the meadow.

"Yeah, I figured as much." William shouted after him, "Just go home and show off that yellow streak all the way down to your posterior."

Mike whirled around. "And you're a jackass. Use your head."

"You're hardly the one to be telling me that," shouted William. Red-faced, he stepped toward him. "After all, you're nothing but a washed-out mama's boy without enough gumption to follow through on something you started."

"And you're so gold-crazy," Mike said. "You're not thinking about tomorrow or what can happen when you do something stupid."

"You're hardly the one to be calling anybody stupid."

Mike shoved him, causing him to trip over a boulder and fall flat on his back.

William picked himself up, jerked off his glasses, and dove for the middle of Mike like a tackle on a football team.

The two of them hit the ground in a tangled mass of arms and legs; kicking, punching, and grabbing at each other's clothes and hair. As they wrestled, they rolled over and over until they smashed against a boulder near the edge of the meadow.

Mike struggled to his feet and grabbed William around the neck in a chokehold as he received a punch in the stomach. They fell over the boulder, and as they hit the ground in a cloud of dust, Mike caught a glimpse of a band of small, white-striped animals scampering out of their way.

Realizing what they were, he panicked. Instead of lying still and letting them wander away, he scrambled to his feet. William did the same. Turning into each other, they banged their heads together and down they went again.

The five skunks, a mother and four half-grown youngsters, swung their tails about like a well-organized team. They shot out one round after another of reeking fluid.

Rubbing the bruise on his head, Mike yelled, scrambled back over the boulder, and ran like a pack of wolves were behind him. William followed, shrieking at the top of his voice. They splashed into the deepest part of the stream, clothes and all. The water seemed to help somehow, but it wasn't enough.

"That smell," gasped Mike. "I can't stand it!" He ducked his head back under the surface.

"My glasses," William exclaimed. "I've got to get my glasses." Sloshing out of the stream, he ran back to where the fight had started. In a moment, he reappeared with his glasses in place.

"Come on," he shouted. "I'm not staying around here."

"Wait up," yelled Mike. He pulled himself out of the water and ran to catch up.

They sliced their way back through the meadow, climbed back over the wall, and dropped to the trail. Dripping wet and without slowing for a breath, they ran past "The Spaniard" toward the horses. As they approached, Cimarron and Big Red snorted, backed away, and rolled their eyes.

"Easy, boy." Mike grabbed Big Red's reins. "Everything's all right."

Big Red didn't seem to agree. Neither did Cimarron. Rearing and neighing, they jerked loose and galloped away.

Mike and William chased them until William tripped over a rock and fell. Out of breath, Mike flopped down next to him and watched as the horses jumped the stream and disappeared over a rise.

CHAPTER 8

The Rescue

Mike guessed right about his father. He and Will were still a couple of miles from the ranch house when two men appeared on horseback. Though some distance away, Mike had no problem picking out his dad.

Mr. Watkins sat erect and hatless on his stallion. He had a citified air about him that distinguished him from his companion.

By contrast, the other rider wore a cowboy hat and boots with a rifle strapped next to his saddle. Mike recognized him as a neighbor from an adjacent ranch.

The horses halted a short distance away.

Mike's dad called out to them. "Hey, are you two all right?"

"Yeah…sort of," said Mike hesitantly.

"We sure could be better," added William.

Mr. Watkins spurred his horse to move closer. However, the black stallion snorted and veered to one side.

"Dad," called Mike. "Wait! There's a problem."

Ignoring his son's plea, Mr. Watkins yelled at the animal. "Hey. You cross-eyed nag. What's wrong with you?" He kicked the sides of his horse, urging it forward. The stallion reared, its eyes wide with fright.

"Dad! No…," Mike shouted. He cringed as his father lost his balance and fell, hitting the ground with a thud.

When Mike and William ran over to him, Mr. Watkins took one whiff and exclaimed, "Great stars above! No wonder! Back off, guys. I'm fine. Just back off!"

The neighbor patted his horse to calm it and started laughing. He laughed so hard that, for a moment, he looked in danger of falling off as well. "Charles," he said, wiping a shirtsleeve across his eyes, "I've got some extra cans of tomato juice you can have."

"Thanks. I'd appreciate it." Mr. Watkins made a face.

Glancing at Mike and William, the rider wiped tears from his eyes as he turned his brown and white pinto toward the ranch house. "Sorry," he gasped, "just can't help it." As he rode off, he added, "Meet you back at the ranch."

Mike hung his head and kicked the gravel at his feet. "Sorry, Dad," he said. He could hear the neighbor laughing a quarter mile down the trail.

"Me too," added William sheepishly.

His father pointed at a nearby stream. "The two of you get those clothes off and see if you can get rid of some of that smell. I'll be back with the soap and tomato juice."

Mike shuffled toward the water while Mr. Watkins remounted his horse. After he had galloped off, Mike pulled the soggy map out of his pocket and slipped it under a rock. Then, he and William piled their clothes on the bank of the stream, and Mike put their cell phone in a dry spot before moving down into the frigid water.

"We really did it this time," said Mike, shuddering as he moved down into the water.

"We may have to remain here for the rest of the summer," William added weakly.

Mike squinched his eyes shut and bobbed his head under the surface as William took his glasses off and laid them on the bank.

"I hope Dad brings us our bedrolls," said Mike, shaking the water out of his hair.

"Sorry," said William quietly. "If I hadn't been so obstinate and getting carried away with wanting to acquire this treasure, we wouldn't be in this predicament."

"It wasn't your fault any more than mine," said Mike. "I kind of lost my temper."

"Yeah, you did, didn't you?" William grinned.

Mike cupped his hand and splashed water at him. "Hey, stupid, you're not supposed to agree with me."

"Oh? I was just being veracious." William splashed back at Mike.

"There you go again."

"I said I was being honest."

"Well, then, say honest."

Mike received a face full of water as an answer. He wiped his eyes.

"All right, you asked for it." Mike held one arm across his eyes and moved toward William, splashing like a madman.

William splashed back in the same way until he decided he had enough. He held up his hands and gasped, "I surrender!"

Mike dropped down until only his head could be seen. "You know, I don't think the smell is so bad if you stay mostly under the water."

"Yeah," agreed William, "but it's too cold to stay long." He laughed.

"What's so funny?"

"I was just contemplating. We won't be able to catch fish in this area for a month full of Sundays. In fact, I doubt if any self-respecting creature would stay in this water for the rest of the summer."

"If they did," Mike added, "they'd taste like skunk juice."

The boys chuckled.

"I can't stand this any longer," said William. He shot up out of the water and pulled himself out on the bank. He shuddered. "L-Look, I'm turning bl-blue."

Mike decided he had enough as well. He followed William out and started shaking.

"Likewise," he chattered, "'cept y-you've just g-got more to t-turn bl-blue than I-I do." He grabbed his shirt and held his breath while drying himself off.

"Looks like we have a choice," said William, grabbing a quick breath. "We either freeze to death or suffocate from the odor."

"There's no skunk like a wet skunk." Mike held his nose.

"You're one to be talking."

"Are you callin' me a wet skunk?"

"You can bet your bushy tail I am."

Mike grabbed William around the neck in a chokehold and started to throw him down.

"Stop!" William yelled. "In my present condition, I'd prefer not to sit on the ground."

"All right." Mike released him and rubbed a bruise on his foot. "We'll put off this match until later—under less trying conditions."

"You don't stand a chance."

"But I owe you one."

"We'll see about that."

The boys looked at each other, laughed, and held their noses.

***

The fun ended when Mr. Watkins returned. Mike and William scrubbed themselves down with tomato juice and soap until their skin turned red and raw. Even then, the treatment didn't take all the smell away.

Mr. Watkins tossed them a couple pairs of old overalls. He dug a hole and picked up their clothes with the end of his shovel. After dropping them in, he shoveled a mound of dirt on top of them.

"You two have a flashlight?" asked Mr. Watkins.

Mike nodded. "We have my small one."

"Guys, I'm sorry about this." Mr. Watkins mounted his horse. He took off his dark glasses and gazed at the boys. "I can't get into this area with the pickup and no self-respecting horse would let you near him. About the only way the two of you can go anywhere is to hoof it. In fact, when you get home, you'd better stay at the bunkhouse for a while. I'll put your bedrolls on the bunkhouse porch." He pulled the key out of his pocket and pitched it to Mike as if he were throwing peanuts to an elephant. He added, "I'd give you a ride, but Ol' Blackie wouldn't go for it."

"I understand, Dad," replied Mike. "We'll be fine."

"Wish we had our bikes," muttered William.

"Sorry I can't help." Mr. Watkins grimaced. He put his glasses back on. "Okay, guys. Hit the road. By the time you get to the bunkhouse, supper ought to be ready. We'll get some food out to you." He nudged his horse and left.

"C'mon, Will," said Mike with a sigh. "We might as well get moving." He frowned. In addition to having a couple of miles yet to walk, they were also to be treated as outcasts.

"Guess so, but—you know—I'm not so sure I want to stay in the same place where Joe…"

"Yeah, I know. Maybe we could sleep in the barn."

"That might work."

William grabbed his glasses, and Mike got his cell phone and the map from under the rock.

***

The sun had already dropped behind the mountain when Mike and William finally arrived at the bunkhouse and flopped down on the steps.

"You know, this place doesn't look near as scary as the other day," said Mike. "I don't think I've got enough energy to get to the barn."

"I agree, but I don't want to go inside. Let's just stay here on the porch," William said in an exhausted voice as he leaned against the handrail.

"Agreed," said Mike.

Soon, Mike's mother arrived with their supper. She handed them each a tray of food. "How are you?" she asked.

"Okay," chorused Mike and William.

Holding her breath, Mother brushed back her dark hair, and gave each of them a big hug. She backed off and made a hasty retreat.

As she headed across the yard, she called back over her shoulder, "Goodnight, you two."

After supper, Mike and William rolled their bedding out on the porch. Mike slipped into his bedroll and fell asleep before he could pull up the zipper.

***

Mike's dad delivered breakfast the next morning. "You know Big Red and Cinnamon got back to the stables all right yesterday."

Mike nodded. "I kind of figured they would."

"What happened, anyway?"

"We were checking out some Indian writings," explained Mike, "when we came on this family of skunks kind of sudden-like. The horses ran off when we tried to get back on them."

"Can't blame 'em for that," said Mr. Watkins.

After Mike's father left, Mike and William sat on the bunk-house steps to mull over their ill-fated experience.

"I figure it'll be a week before the folks'll let us back in the house." Mike sneezed and rubbed his nose.

"A week is a long time," said William. He looked at his bedroll still lying out on one end of the porch. "Maybe we could utilize one of the bedrooms on this end of the bunkhouse."

"Maybe so." Mike still wouldn't want to spend a night in Joe's old room, but one of the other rooms might be better than the porch. "I'm game to try it if you are."

William nodded. They rolled up their bedrolls and went into the bunkhouse. The room nearest the front door smelled a little musty, but it was unoccupied and seemed to be the best choice. Pitching their bedrolls on two of the beds, they sat on the edge of the mattresses.

"It'll probably be a week before Big Red and Cimarron will let us near them," said Mike.

"Mike, we have to do something." William shook his head. "That trail we were on will lead us to the gold. I'm certain of it."

45

"Yeah, you're probably right. I wonder if Joe had found that trail." Mike thought a moment and muttered, "I'd sure like to learn more about that shaman." Through the window, he watched their grandfather walking across the yard to the dusty old ranch pickup. "I think I know just the place to do it. C'mon."

Outside, he yelled, "Hey, Granddad!"

Grandfather Watkins stopped. He scratched his mustache and waited for the boys to catch up to him.

Mike asked, "Where 'bouts are you heading?"

"Into town."

"Could we catch a ride?"

"Why?"

Though his grandfather sounded gruff, the sparkle in his eyes said otherwise. "We need to take back a library book."

"Kind of a sudden interest in the library lately." Granddad raised an eyebrow.

"Not much else to do."

"I can help you on that score," replied Granddad. "Got a fence that needs mending"

"Aw, c'mon, Granddad, that's not what I'm talking about," said Mike. "Will and me...well, we've got a couple of special things we want to find out about."

"Oh, all right. Hop in." Granddad sniffed in their direction. "On second thought, I'm not sure the town of Springer is quite ready for you yet."

Mike began, "We're just going to the library..."

"And we'll stay away from people," finished William.

"Good idea," agreed Granddad, "but you ride in the back."

Mike frowned. Would he and William be regarded as lepers for the rest of their lives—even with their own family? He trotted into the house to get the library book and tell his mother where they were going. When he got back, he and William climbed into the camper on the back of the pickup and settled on the floor behind the cab.

"I'll drop you off in front of the library, and you'll have about ten minutes," called out Granddad. "Then you be out for me to pick you up. All right?"

46

"Okay," chorused William and Mike.

Granddad drove the rattling, old pickup out the drive and turned onto the highway while Mike and William huddled in their jackets for protection from the crisp, morning air.

"Now understand, I'm all for this getting away for a while," said William, "but why the library? We don't need to return this book for another couple of weeks."

"We need to find out more about this shaman guy. He might know something about Joe's accident. Why would he show up at the funeral like he did? Then there's this wolf business." Mike stuck his hand out a side window of the camper, moving it around in the wind like the wing of an airplane.

"All right, I understand. But what's the library got to do with it?" William lay back in the bed of the truck and put his feet up against the cab.

"Maybe nothing." Mike flopped down next to William. He put his hands behind his head and imitated his cousin's position.

"Then why go?"

"Look, Will, if we ask Granddad too much stuff, he'll wonder what we're up to."

"So?"

"So who else knows even more than Granddad about what goes on around here?"

"All right, I'll bite," said William. "Who?"

"Why Roscoe, of course—the all-knowing, all-seeing city librarian."

CHAPTER 9

A Clue

The truck turned off the interstate onto the highway leading into Springer. William fell over on top of Mike, knocking the wind out of him.

"Hey…get off."

William scrambled back into a sitting position. "Mike, I doubt what Roscoe will tell us will be the truth. He's one of those people who thinks he's an authority on everything."

"Well, yeah…" Mike gasped for air. "But he's been around a long time…and he keeps up on all the gossip. He's bound to know something about this shaman."

The truck turned onto Main Street and pulled up in front of the library. Granddad called back, "I'll probably be waitin' out front when you're done. Just got one little item to pick up at the drug store."

Mike and William climbed out the back, waved, and raced into the building.

"Well…howdy, boys? Heh heh heh. Back already?" Roscoe Sweeney sat at his usual place behind the checkout counter. He peered at them from behind a magazine he was holding in front of him.

"Thought we'd return that book we checked out," Mike announced as he set the book firmly down on the counter in front of him.

"Oh? Find anything interesting?"

"Sure, there's a lot of stuff in it." Mike laid the book on the counter. "Say, I was wondering what you might know about an Indian around these parts. He's called *the shaman* by most folks."

"*The shaman*, you say." Roscoe closed his magazine. "Must be that old Apache that lives somewhere up on the mountain. Nobody knows exactly where...'cept maybe the Indian woman named Karana." Suddenly, he sniffed the air suspiciously and gazed about him as if looking for the source of an odor. Finally, he shrugged and stared at the boys over his glasses.

"Where does this Karana live?" asked William.

"She's got a place on the plateau just west of your grandfather's ranch." Roscoe squinted at them. "How come this sudden interest in Indians?"

"The shaman was at Joe's funeral," explained William. "He said something about a white wolf."

The librarian laughed and got to his feet. His owlish eyes magnified through the lenses and Mike thought about the story of little Red Riding Hood. When Riding Hood said, "Grandma, what big eyes you have," Roscoe could respond, "The better to see inside your head and discover what you're up to."

"Well," said Roscoe, "if you go with everything you hear, the shaman is the leader of a band of Apaches that still believe in wolf worship. Most Indians gave up that sort of thing years ago, but it's said this tribe still does it every month at the full moon. They meet at a place somewhere up on Lookout Mountain where they dance around a fire and use live sacrifices. Heh heh heh. I'd say you two might be just about the right size to be their guests on some bright, moonlit night."

Mike gulped.

William said nothing. He just stared out the window as if zapped by a wizard and frozen on the spot.

"Will," said Mike, "let's go back and look...for..."

William kept staring out the window.

"Will," repeated Mike. He grabbed his cousin's shoulder. "Hey, are you all right?"

William snapped out of it. "Awesome," he exclaimed. "That's it. The Circle of Fire!"

"What circle?" snapped Roscoe.

"Oh, he's just talking about a picture we found," said Mike quickly. "It's not important." He tugged at William. "C'mon, we don't have long, you know. Granddad will be waiting."

"Oh, yeah," said William. "Thanks, Mr. Sweeney."

"Sure, I guess." Roscoe frowned. He added, "Oh, by the way, how about opening that window. I think we've got a family of skunks that must've moved back under the building again."

"Yes, sir," said William hastily. "We'll take care of it." He didn't say anything else until they had opened the window and moved in among the books. They crouched in a row between shelves near the back of the library. He whispered, "Mike, that drawing in the cave?"

"Yeah, you're right," agreed Mike. "It was a 'circle of fire' with animals outside it—probably wolves."

"And eating whatever was left for a sacrifice," said William with a shudder.

"Or whoever," added Mike.

William headed for the computer.

"Where're you going?"

"There's got to be a book on Indians that'll tell us about this wolf business. This all fits, and I want to know more about it." William scrolled through several frames until he slowed to a stop. "Yeah. Here we go. A book on Apaches."

He headed for the nonfiction section. Pulling the book from the shelf, he sat cross-legged on the floor and began flipping through its pages.

Mike wasn't sure a book would be of much value. It would take more than a study of the history of Apaches to understand it all, but he wasn't about to tell that to William.

William stopped at a chapter on ceremonies. "Look, here it says, 'The Apache referred to the wolves as their brothers. The broth-

50

ers were greatly admired because of their cunning, strength, and endurance. Special rituals and ceremonies given in honor of this animal were known to occur with the earliest groups of nomads on the North American continent.'"

He continued to flip through the pages. Finally, he sighed and returned the book to the shelves. "It doesn't give any particular tribe, and there's nothing about a Circle of Fire."

"Still," added Mike, "it tells us something."

"What?"

"That Apaches worshipped wolves, and maybe for once, Roscoe knew what he was talking about." He chuckled, "C'mon, Granddad will be looking for us."

Mike remembered Roscoe's comment about the skunks and steered William in a wide circle past the librarian's desk.

"Hey, going so soon?" said Roscoe. "Heh heh heh. Find any more maps?"

"No, afraid not," said William. "We have to go. See you."

They rushed out the door. Out front, Granddad was waiting. They hopped into the camper and waved at him through the rear window.

On the way back to the ranch, Mike asked, "Will, did you tell Roscoe anything about the map?"

"Of course not."

"I wonder why he asked if we'd found any more of them?"

William frowned. "Maybe he eavesdropped on some of our conversations."

"Yeah, maybe," agreed Mike as he rubbed his chin and stared out the window.

"I wonder how far from the ranch this Karana woman lives."

Mike shrugged. "Granddad will know."

The boys rode quietly for the rest of the trip. After they hopped out of the pickup, Mike walked up to his grandfather. "Thanks for the lift."

"You're welcome."

Mike shuffled from one foot to the other. "We're wondering about something."

"What's that?"

"The librarian said something about a real Indian living near us somewhere."

Granddad Watkins tugged on his mustache before he answered. "Must be talking about Karana."

"Yeah, that's her name. Where does she live?" asked William.

"A couple miles west just off the highway. It's up on the plateau—the old Radisson Place."

"Is she very friendly?" asked Mike.

"Don't know. She doesn't have much to do with anybody. I heard she herds a bunch of goats up there."

"Thanks, Granddad," said Mike with a grin.

A few minutes later, Mike and William were on their way. They followed the trail west from the ranch house, heading down the dusty back road toward the ledge named Lover's Leap located at the entrance to Cimarron Canyon. Mike remembered seeing the old Radisson Place up on the ridge from the road across the canyon.

"I'm not sure about this," said William uneasily. "From the description Granddad gives, this old Indian woman is probably none too amiable."

"She's probably not very friendly either," Mike said innocently. "Maybe she's just lonely. How does anybody know if they haven't met her?"

William opened his mouth to say something then seemed to think better of it. He rolled his eyes. Shaking his head, he turned and trudged on up the road.

As they got near the northern slope, they found a trail leading through the forest and up a steep incline toward the plateau. Mike chose the shorter route. The only other way followed a winding paved roadway up to the plateau and past the front gate of the Radisson Place about a mile to the south.

After they had climbed a while, William, who had been dragging behind, yelled, "Stop!" He flopped down against the trunk of a stately pine. "I think maybe we should have taken the highway."

"Yeah?" said Mike, backtracking down the trail to where William was sitting. "Don't you remember that high fence up on the road with the 'No Trespassing' sign?"

"What would you call that?" William pointed.

Mike glanced up at the barbed wire fence running along the edge of the plateau. "Aw, come on Will. We've climbed through worse than that," he said, moving toward it.

William sat with his mouth open.

"What's wrong?" asked Mike. He turned to see what William was staring at.

Ahead, beyond a place where the trail met the fence, the skull of a human skeleton leered at them from a post. The shaft of an arrow protruded from an eye socket where it had passed through it and the back of the skull into a tree. Tacked below the skull was a sign that read "No Trespassing."

CHAPTER 10

The Old Radisson Place

William ran halfway to the bottom of the trail before Mike caught up to him. He grabbed the back of William's belt and pulled him to a stop.

"Whoa, wait a minute."

"You wait!" puffed William. "There is no way… I am going… over that fence."

"Will, that's just a setup…to scare people away."

"It does a first-rate job."

"Aw, c'mon," Mike pleaded. "We've got to go. We've come all this way…and it's still daylight."

"No way!" William flopped down on the trail.

"You aren't scared, are you?" said Mike, scowling down at him.

"Course not, but…but…common sense says you don't go fooling around with dead folks. That's not just a dead animal up there. That's a real, live, human skull!"

"Will, what're you talking about?" said Mike. "It's only a bone. We've got to find this Karana woman." He squatted so he could gaze directly into his cousin's eyes. "Come on now. We've got to figure out where the Circle of Fire is and what all of this has to do with Joe and the gold."

"I know precisely where that gold is, and you do too." William frowned.

"Maybe." Mike stood up. "But not for sure. Besides, what can this one Indian woman do? I bet she's just an old hag without any teeth. She probably has to gum down everything she eats."

"I don't care." William pointed at the clouds gathering on the upper levels of Lookout Mountain. "Besides, it's going to rain."

"That's no excuse. We've got plenty of time to get there and back." Mike glared at his cousin. The time had come to take a stand. "I'm going, and if you're too scared to go with me, stay here. Go on home if you want." He turned and began trudging up the trail.

He almost got out of hollering range and began to worry his bluff hadn't worked when suddenly, William yelled, "Wait a minute."

Holding in a sigh of relief, Mike halted. He sat on a boulder while William puffed up the trail toward him.

"All right! I'm here, but you lead the way." William caught a big breath of air.

Mike crawled through the fence, and William followed. They skirted around the skull in a wide circle, returned to the trail, and continued.

The woods seemed to thicken as the shadows grew longer. The silence weighed down the air around them as they made their way toward the center of the plateau. The birds no longer sang. Even the leaves stopped their rustling.

Mike's heart thumped heavily in his chest. He had never been in a stretch of woods this quiet. He looked above. The clouds were building fast as if rushing to close in and trap them.

William breathed heavily along behind him. "Mike," he spluttered, "how much further?"

"Don't know," gasped Mike, "but it can't be far."

They stepped into a clearing, and the old Radisson Place loomed before them. The vines and bushes were so thick the house's size couldn't be determined with a casual glance. Nearby, an aged barn stood defiantly against the ravages of weather with an opening into a fenced-in pasture.

William seized Mike's arm, and Mike jerked away like a gremlin had snatched at him. "I wish you'd stop that." He whispered. "This place is creepy enough without you grabbing me."

"This place, it…it doesn't feel right."

"I agree, but we're here." Mike peered at the dark shadows building around them and added, "Let's get moving."

They moved toward an old picket fence as the ghostly stillness blanketed the woods like the insides of a mausoleum. The fence reminded Mike of an old cemetery he had once stumbled into while wandering through a field on a Texas prairie. Inside that dismembered fence had been a group of broken headstones and sunken graves.

He glanced behind him. Eyes seemed to be watching; eyes from deep in the woods; unblinking eyes that stared straight into him.

The sun disappeared behind a cloud, and Mike shivered. He lifted a rusty latch and shoved on the squeaky, half-broken gate. William froze as a sudden gust of wind swirled a batch of dead leaves about them like a flurry of frightened sparrows.

Mike blinked and rubbed his eyes. The house seemed empty. There were no curtains, and in spite of the vines and bushes, he could see through the windows. He peered through dusty, cracked glass into dark rooms with scant furniture and barren walls.

"Doesn't look like anybody's here," he whispered. "C'mon, let's check out the barn."

William crouched low next to the bushes and followed Mike toward the corner of the house.

The barn stood in the back, about fifty yards away. The huge, weather-beaten structure had a double door in the front and a small door on one side opening into a corral containing a herd of white goats.

William stepped through a broken section of the fence that surrounded the house. Mike followed him to the corral and stared through the rails at the restless animals.

He shuddered. The barn stood like an ominous and forlorn structure defying anyone to approach it. He didn't really know why, but he had to look inside.

"Why would an Indian woman keep a herd of goats?" asked William. He shook his head.

"Wolf-bait maybe," whispered Mike.

"Yeah, that's food for thought."

Suddenly, a low growl came from somewhere nearby. The sky darkened as the goats crowded against each other into a far corner of the corral.

"That was no goat," said Mike.

"Let's back off," whispered William, "slowly."

The boys backed away from the corral, then turned and ran for the woods.

"Wait!" Mike grabbed William and pulled him to a halt behind the trunk of a tree. "Let's see if anything's following us."

The boys stood still and peered around the trunk. Hearing and seeing nothing, Mike led William back to a place where they could stand in the shadows.

The clouds grew heavier, and a light breeze stirred. A low rumble warned of a developing storm. Again, Mike stared at the barn across the clearing. It housed a secret. He felt sure of it.

"Come on, Will. Let's take a quick look inside that barn. If nobody's there, we'll be on our way."

"Make it fast," William muttered. He looked at the sky. "I want to vacate this place before all Hades breaks loose."

They sprinted across the clearing. At the barn door, Mike motioned to stop.

"What's wrong?"

"Shh. Listen." Mike placed a finger against his lips.

Again, they heard the same sound as before—a deep-throated, far-off growl—as if some large animal warned them to be on their way. The boys looked all about, unable to figure where the sound came from. Mike put his hand on the door handle and pushed it open a crack.

At first, he couldn't see anything. Then as his eyes got used to the gloom, he made out the stalls and stacked bales of hay or grass. In one stall, an old gray mule munched silently while staring at him with wide, curious eyes.

"It's just an old jackass," he whispered. Opening the door a little further, he let out a sigh of relief.

With William close behind him, he slipped inside.

Mike wrinkled his nose. Obviously, goats were kept in the barn as well as in the corral. High walls separated the animals from their feed.

Without warning, a blinding flash of light lit up the barn. The side door flew open as a blast of thunder shook the rafters, and a large, white wolf appeared. His lips curled back in a snarl, and his eyes glowed like burning embers.

Mike gasped, and William stumbled backward. As the lightning flashed again and the thunder roared, both of them yelled at the same time and raced out of the barn.

Mike ran faster than he ever had before. He dashed across the meadow just a step ahead of William. In a moment, however, William zoomed past, screeching and puffing as if the devil himself were on his heels.

"Wait up!" yelled Mike.

But William didn't slow down. He plowed through the woods like a bulldozer with Mike right behind him. Paying no attention to the trail, the two of them crashed down the mountainside, running into fallen trees and stumbling over stumps and rocks.

They tore their clothes on the branches of the trees and scratched their arms while climbing through the barbed wire fence. Reaching the bottom of the slope, they flopped down on the road, gasping for air.

Mike stared at the sky. His chest heaved and sweat stung his cuts and scratches. With restless rumbles and flickering flashes of lightning, the mass of clouds moved past them and across the prairie as the wind died to a whisper.

"M-Mike," William stuttered. "Do you think…" he gulped, "that was her?"

"What? Who?"

"That…that wolf. Do you think that was Karana?"

"Course not," Mike answered between gulps of air. "Where'd you ever get an idea like that?"

"She's a shaman's woman. Maybe she's an Indian witch, one who can change herself into a wolf."

"I don't know what kind of ghost stories you've been reading, but that was no person." Mike shook his head. "That was a real, live wolf."

"But…," insisted William, "the storm—the way that wolf appeared. It was—was unreal."

The howl of a wolf echoed through the valley.

"There's nothing unreal about that." Mike jumped to his feet. "Let's get out of here!"

William didn't have to be told twice.

After the boys returned to the bunkhouse, Mike's father came over to invite them to have supper with the rest of the family.

"Thanks," said Mike. "We'll wash up and be right there."

"Do we have to?" asked William after Mr. Watkins had left. "I've become accustomed to where I am, and I have to admit I like it."

"Me too, but we'd better go." Mike headed for the bathroom. He turned on the water. "You know Dad. If we act out of the ordinary, he'll start asking a lot of questions, and I'm not sure he'd like all our answers."

During supper, much to the boys' relief, nobody said anything about their adventure with the skunks. But Granddad did clear his throat to make an announcement.

Mike lifted an eyebrow at William who just shrugged.

"Edna and I have decided to go into Springer this evening for a Bingo Party sponsored by the Elks Lodge. Charles, you and Joan are invited to join us."

Mike's father looked at his wife. "It might be fun."

"But what about the boys?" she asked.

"You don't have to worry about us," said Mike. "We're all right. Will and I can just watch TV and go to bed. You all go and have a good time."

Dad grinned. He winked at the boys and turned toward his wife. "The boys will be fine. Good." Getting no response from Mom, he added, "Then it's settled."

After they had cleared all the dishes from the table, the phone rang. Mike answered and recognized the voice of William's grandmother calling from Texas to check up on him.

"Will," shouted Mike. "It's for you."

While William ran to use the phone in the kitchen, Mike trotted back to the bunkhouse and got his stuff. He moved his things back into the ranch house room he shared with William. Deep in thought, he walked out to the porch and sat on the railing.

The sun was setting behind Lookout Mountain and throwing long shadows across the plains. Looking toward the mountain, Mike considered what William had said. He had never heard of an Indian witch before, and—try as he might—he couldn't believe anyone could turn themselves into a wolf except in books. There had to be a down-to-earth reason for what they had experienced. He shuddered as he remembered the wolf showing up at the barn door like a phantom.

Suddenly, a hand grabbed Mike's shoulder. Startled, he almost fell off the railing.

"Sorry, I didn't mean to scare you." Mr. Watkins chuckled. "Just wanted to let you know we're about ready to leave. You two behave while we're gone, and stay away from skunks, okay?"

"Dad, of course…" Mike began. Then he noticed the twinkle in his father's eyes. He grinned. "We'll be fine. Don't worry."

Later, after the family left, Mike and William sat in the family room and reviewed all the things that had happened since the funeral. They decided if the horses would allow them near, they would ask the folks to let them ride into the north pasture again the next day. They flopped down on the floor in front of the TV and watched a couple of their favorite shows and the beginning of a horror movie. Mike thought how tame the story was compared to what they had been doing in real life.

During a commercial, William suggested, "This is a good time to go back to the bunkhouse and get our bedrolls."

"I already got mine, but I'll tell you what happened if you don't get back before the commercials are over."

"You mean I've got to go over there by myself?"

"Go on," argued Mike. "If you hurry, you won't miss anything."

"Oh, fine. Well, if I must, I must."

"Hey," Mike called after him. "Get my cell phone while you're there. Okay?"

"All right, but it'll cost you." William slammed the screen door behind him.

The commercials finished, and William hadn't returned. Mike knew he would gripe about missing a part of the movie.

In the movie, the hero's girlfriend wandered alone through a dark forest. The hero shouted her name and walked quietly among the trees. He stopped and listened.

From afar, a distant voice called out, "Mike!"

Mike stared at the screen and decided his imagination was working overtime. The hero in the story walked deeper and deeper into the forest.

Suddenly, a car door slammed.

Mike listened, puzzled. The sound came from outside the ranch house. The folks were returning a lot earlier than expected. He got up and trotted to the door as a small car started out of the driveway.

"Let me go!" screamed a muffled voice.

CHAPTER 11

Alone

Mike panicked.

"Will!" he yelled.

He bolted out the front door and jumped off the porch. Plunging into a cloud of dust, he raced down the drive. By the time he reached the paved surface of the highway, the vehicle's taillights had disappeared over a rise.

He shook his head in disbelief. Things like this just don't happen. Could William really have been in that car? He raced back to the porch.

"Will!" he shouted, hoping he would hear an answer.

He stood still and held his breath. The light from their room in the bunkhouse cast an eerie beam into the twilight. Nothing moved, not even the leaves on the trees. The only sounds came from the TV inside the ranch house. He was alone—entirely alone.

He dashed across the yard and into the bunkhouse. The echo of his footsteps followed him across the porch and through the door into the room they had occupied.

Things were a mess. It was almost as bad as Joe's room had been. Drawers jutted out from the dresser, and some of their clothes lay scattered. Mike's first thought was that William had been looking for something—maybe the cell phone.

He knitted his eyebrows into a frown as he saw his phone lying on the stand next to William's bed. This didn't make sense. Why would anyone mess up things like this? They had no money or anything of much value. All those sorts of things were kept in the ranch house. Why would someone want William? Unless…unless he surprised them, and they grabbed him as a hostage.

Mike grabbed his phone and ran back to the ranch house. He raced through the rooms, turning on all the lights as he went. His heart thumped loudly, and beads of sweat gathered on his forehead. He switched off the TV, backed into a corner, and listened.

Nothing.

He had to do something; but what?

A flash of lightning and a rumble of thunder startled him. He pushed himself tighter into the corner and slammed his fist against the wall. "Stop acting like a stupid baby," he yelled at himself. "Will's in trouble, and I've got to help."

The phone! Of course. He'd call his parents.

He punched the pre-assigned button for his father's number and waited. Finally, the voice recorder came on. "Dad, Will's been kidnapped! Please call me as soon as you can." His mind went blank. He couldn't think of anything else to say, so he ended the call. Why was Will kidnapped?

"Wait a minute," he exclaimed. That tingle was attacking his backbone again.

Mike shouted at the walls. "I know what happened." He frowned. "The map! The gold! That's what somebody wanted."

He had left the map stuck in the pocket of his jacket which was in the bunkhouse. Racing out the door, he ran across the yard back to their room. His jacket lay on the floor, the pockets inside out, and the map gone—the map with all his notes and additional markings on it.

Mike picked up the jacket. "Somebody got it." He frowned. "Somebody's got both William and the map."

Again, a flash of lightning startled him. Then another blast of thunder—louder than before—rattled the windows.

"The police, I'll call the police." Holding on to his jacket, he punched in 911 as he sprinted back across the yard to the ranch house. Large drops of rain splattered about him.

Mike stopped under the overhang on the steps and listened as a female voice answered, "911, please hold."

Hold?

Mike couldn't believe it. In his imagination, a hand with a dagger appeared out of the shadows. It rose high in the air, a flicker of light glinting from the blade.

"King's X!" he shouted. "You'll have to wait. Everything's on hold right now." He tapped his foot impatiently.

Finally, the voice spoke again. "911, may I help you?"

"Yes, ma'am. Somebody kidnapped Will, and I'm here by myself, and…"

A flash of lightning struck a tree near the porch, flaring with such brilliance Mike dropped the phone on the concrete steps as his heart was swallowed by his stomach. Something snapped as the lights went out, and a violent blast of thunder shook the house, making the porch vibrate as if it had a life of its own.

Mike grabbed the cell phone and stuck it against his ear.

Nothing. It was as silent as the insides of a tomb.

"Oh, great!" Feeling his way into the kitchen, he moved along the counter to a drawer. He jerked it open and grabbed a flashlight. Switching on the light, he flashed it on the land phone located on the counter and picked up the receiver.

No dial tone.

A gust of wind blew against the window. Hard objects banged against the roof as if someone were chunking rocks at the house. The sound grew louder.

Mike dropped to the floor and huddled against the cabinet. The hail made a deafening roar as it pounded the walls and roof of the old ranch house. He pulled his knees up to his chin and wrapped his arms around his legs as if trying to make himself disappear into the woodwork. Terror clutched at his innards like a giant hand trying to squeeze the forces of life out of him.

He knew fear was his enemy. He had to fight it, and the only way he could do that would be to face it and overcome it. He slammed his fist against the wall.

"Stop," he yelled. "Stop it!"

As if in response to his cry, the hail suddenly quit, and the wind calmed. The rain settled into a steady drone.

Mike scrambled to his feet. He had to do something. His dad might not think of checking his phone for messages, and it could be hours before the folks got home. Anything could happen in that amount of time. He had to get help, but how?

"Where would they take him?" he asked the dark, empty house.

A jumble of thoughts crisscrossed in his mind. The gold, the map, the Circle of Fire. The gold, the shaman, the wolf. The gold, the skunks, the cave, the map. The gold! He shook his head. No matter where his thoughts led, they came back to the gold. What was it that Granddad had said—gold was the root of all evil?

No, that didn't sound quite right, but it was something like that.

"Will knows the trail leading to the Circle of Fire, and they've got our map." He slumped down on the couch. "Whoever's got him will take him with them to find the gold." He jumped to his feet. "They might not wait until morning either."

He knew what the next step would have to be. It was the last thing in the world he wanted to do, but he had no choice.

He put on his jacket and jammed the flashlight into his pocket. The rain still fell, but it had slowed to a drizzle, the kind that could keep going for hours. He stepped into the darkness and trotted up the drive. At the paved road, he switched on his light and turned west. This time, he'd follow the highway.

Lightning flashed across the sky turning the countryside into a mysterious pale blue. He would have to go to the old Radisson Place. He shuddered at the thought of it, but the next nearest ranch was much further. After all, he hadn't really seen the woman called Karana. She could be a nice person, and maybe the wolf was just an old stray sneaking around trying to attack the goats. Karana might even be grateful that he and William had run it off.

He shuddered again. Who was he fooling? That wolf had run them off.

It was a long way to the plateau, much longer than he remembered. The road climbed sharply through a pair of switchbacks.

As Mike trotted up to the plateau, the rain lessened. Nevertheless, by the time he reached the gateway to the Radisson Place, water dripped from his hair and ran down the middle of his back. His jacket wasn't waterproof, and his shoulders were soaked. He gasped for breath, and his legs felt like rubber. His stomach lurched as the road seemed to sway and dance in front of him.

Dropping to his knees, he braced himself against the ground with his hands until his head cleared and staggered to his feet. He moved past the gateway toward the old house.

The narrow road blended into the trees, and his shoes squished on the drive as if he were splashing through a swamp. A pinpoint of light appeared, and he sprinted toward it, gasping and straining. Yet the harder he ran, the more tired his legs felt, and the slower his stride became.

His last hope rested with this Indian named Karana. She would know about the Circle of Fire. He would ask her to call the police or get the shaman to rescue William.

He reached the old picket fence. Breathlessly, he shoved the gate open and stumbled up the steps and across the loose planks of the porch. He leaned against the door, not having the strength to knock.

The door opened, and he almost fell into the room.

He blinked and looked up. An Amazon stood before him. The woman was so tall her head seemed to rest against the top of the doorframe.

He felt dizzy. The doorway, the light from the house, the woman. They began to get all mixed up. They disappeared into a swirling mist as Mike closed his eyes and dropped to the floor.

CHAPTER 12

Karana

When Mike opened his eyes, he felt something soft and cool on his forehead. A tall shadow stood over him. Nearby, a bare bulb hung from the ceiling, its brightness causing him to blink.

"Are you all right?" asked the shadow.

Mike nodded.

"Why do you come?"

"My cousin's been kidnapped, and I've got to find him." Mike squinted in the light, trying to see the figure's face. "Please, Ma'am, I think they've gone to the Circle of Fire. Maybe we can call the police! Maybe the shaman could help!"

The shadow dropped to his side where the light revealed the stony gaze of a young Indian woman. A beaded band crowned her head, and a pair of black braids of hair hung over her shoulders.

She didn't look anything like what he had imagined. She certainly didn't resemble the old hag without any teeth he had described to William. Her eyes amazed him. They were the only parts of her face showing any feeling. The rest looked carved in stone.

"What do you know of the Circle of Fire?" she asked.

"Me and my cousin—he's William—were looking for a pile of gold coins a gang of robbers hid a long time ago. We found a bunch of marks on a cave wall that show them to be near a place called the

Circle of Fire." He sat upright. "You're the person they call Karana, aren't you?"

A moment of silence elapsed before she answered, "I am."

"Then please help. Somebody stole our map. They've got Will. You…you've got to call the police."

"I have no phone."

"Then you…you can contact the shaman, can't you? Maybe he could help."

Karana stood up and stared down at him. "You want me to contact the Diyin? You do not know what you ask."

Mike put his head in his hands. "You…you're my last hope," he pleaded. "I don't know what else to do."

He hated this. He felt scared, mixed-up, and all by himself. A tear rolled down his face. He dropped his hands and looked up at Karana. Let her see his tears. He didn't care.

The tall Indian gazed at him. Her eyes seemed sad.

"Come," she said. "Hurry."

Steadying himself, Mike grabbed a table leg and pulled himself to his feet.

Karana snatched a poncho from a peg behind the door and led Mike to the corral. Pulling the mule from its stall in the barn, she commanded, "Get on."

After Mike mounted, she handed him the reins. "Hold tight."

A light mist fell around them and dripped from the trees as she grabbed the bit and tugged Mike and the mule behind her.

"Do you want my light?" asked Mike.

"It is not needed."

True to her word, Karana seemed to have no problem in winding her way through the dark shadows. Without looking back at him, she spoke, "Tell me more."

Mike started with the day of the funeral when he and William discovered Joe's ransacked room. He told her about the map and how it led to the "Spaniard." While he spoke, the rain ended, and the clouds parted. Beams of moonlight reflected from the wet leaves causing them to shimmer like glistening gems.

After he had narrated about the kidnapping, Karana said, "Your cousin is in much danger."

"I know, but I don't know what to do."

Karana stopped and gazed upward. She turned to him. "You do not understand." She pointed at the sky. "The moon does not hide its face. The time of The Gathering is here. The Brethren know this. There is great danger."

"Brethren?" Mike gulped. "You mean wolves? At the Ring of Fire? Tonight?"

"Perhaps," said Karana. "The Guardian and I have prepared."

"The Guardian?"

"Our Protector—the one who guards my herd."

A memory of the barn flashed through Mike's mind. He gasped. "The wolf."

"Many moons past," continued Karana, "after the white man drove my people into the mountains, the Brethren showed them how to protect themselves. They were taught how to attack their enemy and disappear like the early morning mist. The Brethren revealed ways of finding food when none existed. My people were taught the law of the Great Spirit so all may work and live together. Now, at the fullness of the moon, we gather to honor the Brethren and share what we have."

"You mean—the sacrifices," said Mike with a shudder.

"The herd is for that purpose," said Karana. "The Circle of Fire is at the entrance to the Inner Chambers where spirits of past Brethren abide." She gazed steadily at Mike. "You must swear to keep it secret."

Mike nodded. "Sure. I promise."

"Do not forget," she warned. "Long ago, others entered the chambers, but did not leave."

He gulped. "Like maybe the robbers and the gold—many years ago."

Again, she grabbed the bit of the mule and tugged. "We must hurry."

The path became steep and rocky. However, Karana didn't slow down. Mike clamped his knees against the sides of the mule and threw his weight forward, holding the reins tightly. "Hey, maybe I ought to walk," he suggested.

"No, the way is not easy."

Mike muttered, "You can say that again."

A glow appeared in the sky above him, piercing through a thin layer of clouds that blocked out the stars yet allowed a misty moon to light the way. A hazy valley was occasionally seen through the treetops below. In the moonlight, it became a tapestry of shades and shadows. Nevertheless, it didn't bother him that they were traveling on a steep, narrow path until they came to a great rock sticking out from the side of the mountain.

Mike thought the path would switch back and cut up over the top, but it turned into a narrow ledge and kept going across the face of the rock. He looked down to his right and gasped. They were hundreds of feet above a broad, dim valley.

A small stone, loosened by the mule, clattered off the edge, and Mike shut his eyes tight. He dropped the reins and hugged the mule's neck as though his life depended on it. Once they had crossed the rock, the path reentered the forest. Gasping a sigh of relief, Mike sat back up and grabbed the reins. The wind did not blow, and the only sounds were the mule snorting and the leaves shuffling as they plodded onward. He thought about what might lie ahead, and his stomach muscles tightened with tension. He could hear himself puffing as if he were working as hard as the mule.

They climbed over the summit and moved down the other side of the mountain. Suddenly, rustling sounds came from the forest about them, and the mule became tense.

Karana spoke quietly in the darkness. "The Brethren know we are here. Do not speak and do only as I say."

CHAPTER 13

The Circle of Fire

Mike swallowed hard. He gripped the reins tightly as Karana pulled him and the mule through a valley of rustling sounds and moving shadows. They walked toward a U-shaped nook surrounded by the towering walls of a group of palisades.

A shallow trench arched across the mouth of the nook, and a high knoll covered with rocks and boulders rose in the middle of it like a shadowy mound of lumpy dough hardened under a moonlit sky.

A movement to the side caught Mike's eye. Flitting shadows sneaked in and out through the underbrush and mingled among the silhouettes of the trees. The shadows stayed away but not far.

He shuddered and wondered if William came this way. Maybe William wasn't even here. Maybe he shouldn't be either.

The moon shone brightly, reflecting on the sandy area around the trench and in the nook. The dusty ground looked worn as if trod on regularly by many feet. A few scattered bones lay about, but there were no skulls or anything showing what sort of creature had been there.

Karana stopped at a dry gully along one side of a palisade. Its rocks were worn smooth from countless seasons of wind and rain. She motioned him to dismount. "Come."

Glad to oblige, Mike scrambled off the back of the mule.

Karana pointed to the gully, and he began to climb. She followed, pulling the mule behind her. Halfway to the top, she shouted, "Wait." Jerking a couple of wide boards from a crack in rocks, she blocked the gully behind them by sliding the boards across the path and firmly fitting them into notches. "Here we are safe."

Mike shrugged his shoulders. The trail was getting awfully steep, probably too much for wolves anyway. Maybe it was just an additional safety precaution.

Karana tied the mule to a bush and motioned on ahead. "We climb."

The way became steeper. In places, Mike had to haul himself up, hand over hand, digging his feet into the crevices and grasping whatever firmly embedded object he could find. When he reached the top, he discovered he had arrived on a ridge next to the pinnacle of a palisade. Karana stepped up behind him.

Mike glanced down at the nook far below. "I don't understand," he said. "Why are trenches dug across that clearing?"

"When the time is right, my people come. They fill the channels with oil and light them with a torch," explained Karana.

Mike scratched his head. "Why?"

"When the ceremonies finish, the fire fades. The Brethren enter to celebrate our good fortunes."

Mike shuddered as he imagined the wolves leaping over the dying flames and attacking the herd of goats brought there for the sacrifice. He saw dark shadows moving about in the valley. "Hope Will isn't down there somewhere."

Karana watched and listened intently. "Something is not right." She pointed toward the mound. "The Brethren gather."

Dark shadows were moving slowly in the cove.

"Why?" asked Mike. A pang of fear tightened the muscles in his chest. "Why are they sneaking around like that?"

"Someone has entered the Inner Chambers."

"Where?"

Karana pointed at the top of the mound. "The entrance is there."

"Maybe it was Will and the guy who captured him."

Karana stood silently for a moment. When she spoke, her voice sounded sad. "Then we are too late."

"What do you mean?" asked Mike. "We'll just go and find them."

"No!" replied Karana sharply. Softly, she added, "Only the shaman enters the home of the Brethren's ancestors. Others who intrude may never leave."

Mike couldn't believe it. He leaped to his feet. "Look, Will is not just my cousin. He's my friend, and…and he's family. I can't just sit up here when he might be in some kind of trouble." He started climbing back down the way they had come.

"No!" shouted Karana. "You do not understand. You cannot go. It is the Guardian's lair. He will take your spirit."

Mike ignored her. He slid down the trail, scattering rocks as he went. William needed him. He couldn't let some old Indian superstition keep him away. William would help if things were reversed.

He heard Karana's voice calling from the ridge. "Stop. Come back!"

Mike ran past the mule to the boards blocking the trail. He climbed upon them and dropped down on the other side.

At the bottom of the gully, he stopped. He heard a low, rumbling growl and saw a pair of shadows running toward him in the moonlight.

He glanced toward the mound and knew he had little choice.

Racing for his life, Mike dashed across the open ground and leaped for a boulder. He heard a snarl, and a pair of jaws snapped behind him. Jerking his feet up, he scrambled to a ledge and looked at his pant leg. A missing piece of it hung out of the mouth of a large gray shadow below him. Another shadow joined the first.

Snapping and growling, they tore the cloth to shreds as Mike clawed his way across the face of the Lookout Mound. He reached a series of roughed out steps spiraling upward around the mound to a narrow opening near the top. Gasping for breath, he climbed to the entrance and stepped inside. Here, the darkness smothered him like the blackness of space. He jerked out his flashlight and beamed it around the small enclosure. On one side, a passage led downward between the boulders.

"Guardian's Lair...huh, I bet," he muttered, "more likely the resting place of a ton of gold. I wonder if Will is all right." He listened. There were no voices or sounds of any kind, only silence. Following the beam of his flashlight, he moved into the passage. He followed it downward, spiraling at a steep angle just like the outside steps had spiraled upward. However, the distance was much greater than the climb on the outside. The walls became clammy, and the air felt cool and damp.

He entered a huge cavern, so large his light couldn't reach the opposite wall. On the floor of the cavern, there were boulders and columns extending toward the ceiling. A muffled roar echoed from the far side. Mike had trouble imagining what it could be. The roar grew louder as he moved along the path weaved among the rocks. He came to the edge of an underground lake. Directing his beam along a cavern wall, he traced a stream of water to its noisy source. An underground waterfall poured from an opening near the ceiling of the cavern.

Suddenly, someone grabbed him from behind. "Well, well... heh heh heh...look who's here."

CHAPTER 14

The Lost is Found

Mike dropped the light. Leaving the jacket in his captor's hands, he tore himself free, whirled around, and swung a hard kick at the man's shins. Feeling it strike home, he snatched his light off the ground and stumbled back up the path.

Roscoe clutched his leg and yelled out a stream of profanity.

With heart pounding, Mike scrambled over a boulder and switched off his flashlight. He peered back over the top of the huge rock. A bobbing glow from a light, and Roscoe's pear-shaped figure appeared. The librarian muttered to himself as he puffed up the path.

Though Mike couldn't make out all of his words above the roar of the waterfall, he couldn't be wrong about the anger on the man's face. He waited until Roscoe had passed the boulder, and the light had faded into the distance before dropping back to the path. He switched on his flashlight. The beam was weak, and he had to squint to see anything. Where was William? Maybe Roscoe had a partner who was holding him prisoner.

Mike didn't dare call out. He would have to explore the cave carefully and quietly. The path ahead split in opposite directions near the edge of the lake. To his left, the trail had two sets of footprints. One set appeared to be smaller than the other and only the larger footprints returned.

Mike whispered, "William." Shining the light low in front of him, he followed the footprints along the edge of the lake toward the falls. Near the falls, the footprints led into a narrow tunnel where the walls widened into another smaller cavern. Here, the sound of the falls faded, leaving the cavern as quiet as a cathedral. The walls curved like the insides of a giant bell. They were smooth and covered with sketches of horses, warriors, bears, and deer.

Mike stared at the figures and traced his finger over the nearest one. At first, he thought they were just a meaningless group of drawings. However, when he studied them more closely, he could tell they connected to make a story. For a moment, he felt as if he had stepped from the present into the long ago, a place where he didn't belong. On the wall to his left, men on horseback were defeating a band of frightened Indians. The Indians looked starved, and the battle seemed unfair. On the wall to his right, the Indians were winning over their enemies and getting ready for a great feast.

A large picture appeared on a distant part of the wall between the two sets of drawings, but Mike couldn't make out the details. He shook his light to make it brighter and moved closer. The picture took shape, and he froze. An exact likeness of the Guardian stared at him. The great phantom wolf appeared much bigger than life. The image was so well drawn the animal's eyes seemed to stare at him as if it were watching his every move.

Mike gasped and stepped backward. He tripped over a stone and dropped his light. It went out, plunging the cavern into total darkness. Falling to his knees, he felt about on the ground. He found the flashlight, picked it up, and slapped it against the palm of his hand.

Nothing happened.

He flipped the switch off and on, then slapped in his palm again…still nothing. His knees shook in the darkness that covered him like a heavy, smothering blanket. He could think of only one thing to do. He would yell until Roscoe found him and take his chances from there.

Filling his lungs with air, he almost screamed, but a faint noise sounded not far in front of him. He stopped, let his air out slowly,

76

and listened. The noise resembled a sob and came from the general direction of where he had seen the painting of the wolf. Crawling on all fours and feeling the ground in front of him, he moved forward. As the sound grew stronger, he could hear the sobs more clearly.

He stopped, puzzled. Now the sound seemed to echo from the ceiling. He called out, "Will, Will, is that you?"

The sobbing stopped.

"Mike? Mike! Where are you?"

Mike started crawling. "I… I don't know exactly. My light's out. Just keep talking. I'll find you."

"No!" said William. "Don't come any closer. You'll fall."

The warning came too late.

CHAPTER 15

Trapped

"Mike, Mike!"

Drops of water splattered in his face, and Mike opened his eyes with a start. He closed them again as his head pounded like the throbbing beat of galloping horse's hooves.

He heard the scratch of a match and gazed in the direction of the sound. The light from a torch almost blinded him, and a pair of hands tugged at his shoulders. He turned his head from the light and groaned.

"Stay here," instructed Will. "I'll be right back."

How stupid, thought Mike. I'm not going anywhere. He fought to clear his head. "Got to get moving," he muttered. He pushed himself up on his elbows and began drawing in a big breath of air when a wet shirt hit him in the face, knocking him flat again. He grabbed it off his face and sat up. "What're you trying to do?"

Shirtless, William flopped down in front of him. His glasses were missing, and he still sobbed a little, but he grinned through his tears. "You can't know how great it is to hear you gripe."

"Aw, I'm all right," said Mike gruffly, rubbing his head with the wet shirt. He felt bad about yelling at him. Shielding his eyes, he looked at William. "Where are your glasses?"

"I lost them somewhere," said William with a shrug. He raised the torch and pointed. "You fell from up there. How'd you find me, anyway?"

"It was kind of a guess. You remember when we were looking for Karana?"

"Yeah."

"Well, I found her, and she's not exactly what you think. She brought me to you—sort of."

"Where is she?"

"She's outside…but that's another story." Mike rubbed his bruises and looked up at the ledge. He figured it to be about the height of three six-foot men placed one on top of another. Encircling them was a solid wall of jagged rock. "Where are we?"

"Something Roscoe called a sinkhole."

"He kidnapped you from the bunkhouse," Mike stated. "Why?"

"I came across him about the time he found the map," said William as he helped Mike to his feet. "Since he couldn't let me tell everybody what he was doing, he decided to take me along. After we got here, he tied a rope around my waist and lowered me in this place while he went searching for the gold."

"The gold," Mike said excitedly. "Is it really here?"

"Roscoe thinks it is—and actually, so do I—though I tried to convince him otherwise." William frowned. "It didn't work."

Mike grabbed the torch. "Why didn't you have this lit while I was up there looking for you? I sure could have found you a lot easier."

"I had no way to light it," said William. "You have the matches, remember? I just now got them out of your pocket." He added, "One curious thing though."

"What's that?"

"The torch was already here…like…like someone had left it on purpose. I found it when I was feeling along the wall looking for a way out."

Mike tossed William's shirt back to him. "That means…"

"Someone's been here before," said William.

Mike decided maybe things weren't as dark as they had seemed. If someone got in to leave a torch, there had to be a way out. "Where'd you find the water?"

William wrung out his shirt and looped it through the belt around his waist. He nodded toward the center of the sinkhole. "Over there."

Mike pulled himself to his feet. His head still ached, but he couldn't be worried about that now. He lifted the torch high. They were in a big hole all right. A small pool of water filled in the center surrounded by rocks and boulders that might have fallen from the floor above.

"Kind of a mess, isn't it?" he said. "Let's see if we can find how the torch bearer got in here." He studied the walls of their prison. In spite of feeling like he had been run over by a truck, he wasn't going to complain. They were alive. He pointed toward a hole in one wall. "Let's see where it goes."

William clawed his way up to it and peered inside.

"Doesn't go anywhere," he called out. "It's just a dead end."

"Well, come on back down. There's got to be a way out somewhere."

William dropped down to join Mike, and they started exploring the walls of their prison. Finally, after they had investigated the entire perimeter of the sinkhole, Mike sat down on a boulder. He gazed at the jagged edges of the hole above them and muttered, "There's got to be a way."

William cupped his hands in the pool of water to get a drink. "Mike!" he exclaimed. "Listen."

The sound of water rippling across the stones came from behind a large boulder.

Mike shrugged. "So?"

"Let's take a look."

Holding the torch before him, Mike moved toward the rock. William slid along the side of the boulder. "The water," he exclaimed, "it echoes behind this rock...like...maybe there's a tunnel or passage."

Mike held the torch above a space between the rock and the wall. The flames fluttered. "Must be some sort of opening back there. Let's see if we can move this rock enough to get through."

After wedging the torch into a crack on the wall, he and William shoved on the rock, inching it out far enough to let them squeeze behind it. Mike grabbed the torch, and they crawled into a low, narrow passage. Water trickled through the rubble below their feet and the sound of it faded as it seeped away to some unknown destination. The passage tapered downward.

Mike's eyes burned, and he coughed from the smoke given off by the torch. He passed it back to William. "Here," he spluttered, "take this thing. I'm going to see if I can move some of these stones out of the way."

"Careful," warned William. "They look…"

For the second time inside an hour, his warning came too late. The rubble shifted beneath his feet, and the torch went out plunging their surroundings into the blackness of a tomb as they tumbled to the bottom of a long slide. Both of them coughed and choked from the dust. They groped about until they found each other.

"Still got the torch?" Mike gasped.

"Naw, lost it."

"It ought to be near."

After a moment of silence, William yelled, "Mike!"

"What?"

"I… I think I just found a bone."

"Where are the matches?"

"You got them, remember…to light the torch."

"Oh, yeah."

After a moment of shuffling, William struck a match, and immediately, Mike regretted it. They both screamed at the same time.

Next to William lay a human skeleton. The skull faced toward them. Its eyeless sockets staring at them above a toothless jaw.

William dropped the match.

CHAPTER 16

The Gold

"The torch," Mike shouted. "We've got to find the torch." His heart pounded like he had finished a marathon.

William struck another match.

Mike refused to look at the skeleton. He saw the torch lying on a rock above William's head and grabbed it. Holding it toward William, he said, "Here, light the end!"

William struck another match and held it below the torch's head. "Hey, all right." He said, a tinge of relief in his voice as the match's tiny flame blossomed.

Mike concentrated on the torch, turning it slowly until the flames took a good hold. "For being around such a long time, it sure burns well," he said casually.

William said nothing. He gazed beyond Mike, his face whiter than usual, and his eyes wide.

Mike wheeled around and gasped.

Skeletons! Not just a few, but a chamber full. Some were lying against the wall as if in life they had been searching for a way out. Others must have given up. They lay in positions against the rocks as if they had just waited—waited to die.

Mike struggled to his feet. Would his fate be the same? *No*, he thought to himself. He couldn't let his thoughts go in that direction. They would find a way out and they had nothing to fear. After all, he thought, these were only the bony frames of what had been but were no more.

He and William moved slowly among the skeletons. Much of the clothing had rotted away, but, here and there, scattered sheds of tan peeked out among the bones. Strange, they should all have bits of the same cloth—as if dressed the same way.

"Will!" Mike stopped and pointed at a larger piece of the material. "It's them, it's the robbers."

"Could be," said William, sounding somewhat hesitant.

"Could be? Ha, I know it is," said Mike. "They were all wearing those coats."

"You mean dusters," interrupted William.

"Yeah…whatever…but that means…"

"Sure. The treasure!"

"It's got to be here too." Mike held the torch high.

"Let's get to looking," exclaimed William.

Stalactites hung from the ceiling; some as thin as straws, others as thick as great pillars. From the floor, several stalagmites shot upward like the blades of knives. In some places, stalactites and stalagmites had joined to form columns. Most of the skeletons were in the rear of the cavern among fallen columns and broken stalagmites. Debris cluttered the floor, and large chunks of rock partly covered some of the bony remains.

Mike held the torch high. "Look."

A large hole appeared overhead in this part of the area where a whole section of the ceiling had caved in.

"So that's what happened," said William.

"Yeah, the floor must have given way while they were walking."

"It explains the torch. One of the survivors must have left it when trying to find his way out. But where did they hide the gold?"

"They didn't." Mike nodded toward the center of the debris.

One skeleton, partly hidden under a huge pile of rock, had the top of a bag in his bony grasp. The bag had ripped open on one side, and its scattered contents rested among the rocks.

"Wow!" Mike picked up a ten-dollar gold piece and held it close to the torch.

"Awesome!" William shouted. He dug both hands into the bag and lifted out a pile of coins.

Nearby were two more bags. Mike jammed the torch between a pair of rocks and checked them out. They were stuffed with more gold coins.

"Mike, we're rich."

"Yeah?" Mike replied. "There's only one problem. How're we going to get it out?"

A beam of light flashed down on them and a voice called from above. "Heh heh heh. Maybe I can help."

"Roscoe!" Mike exclaimed.

"Yeah, think you're a pretty smart kid, eh? Thanks for finding it. As for taking it out, I've got just the thing."

Roscoe laughed again and jerked a small pistol from his coat pocket. He tossed down one end of a rope. "Tie this around one of those bags."

Leaving the one bag in the grasp of the skeleton, Mike slowly looped the rope around the top of another hefty one. Things were not looking all that great right now. He wondered just how far Roscoe might go to make sure there were no witnesses left to lay claim to the treasure. "What about us? What're you going to do with us?"

"Why nothing." Roscoe laughed again. "I'm not going to bother you in the least. You just help me get this gold out, and in return I won't have to use this little pistol of mine."

William helped Mike tie the rope. He whispered, "We don't have much choice, do we?"

"It's tied," Mike announced.

Roscoe stuck the pistol in his belt. With a grunt, he jerked the rope tight and pulled the bag up the wall of the cavern.

"Mr. Sweeney, we're trapped," called Mike. "Could you at least leave us the rope?"

Roscoe set the bag between his feet and began untying it. He breathed so hard he could barely talk, and he laughed between gasps. "Heh heh. Don't see why—with all the company you got down there—it'd be rude to leave them so soon." He puffed a little and laughed again. "After all, they've been waiting around a long time for guests." He opened the bag and ran his fingers through the gold coins. "Yeah, that's more like it."

Roscoe retied the bag and lifted it. He flashed his light on the boys and laughed. "Don't go anywhere. I'll be right back."

CHAPTER 17

Escape

"There's got to be a way out of here," said Mike grabbing the torch. "This light isn't going to last us forever."

"Roscoe will be back soon." William grunted as he climbed over a boulder. "With that load, he won't travel far."

"He'll never get past the entrance anyway," Mike announced over his shoulder. The torch burned low, and he held it high as he walked along one wall.

"Why?"

"Wolves."

"What wolves?"

"You didn't see them when you came in?"

"We heard some wild animals sneaking around, but we never saw them." William stopped before a huge crack on the face of a wall. "Roscoe figured they'd disappear after he forced me into the passage."

"Well, they didn't."

"It's a long way to his jeep," said William. "Even if he could maneuver past the wolves, he'd have to haul those bags one by one down the side of the mountain."

Mike gulped as he remembered a story about how some guy gave himself to a lion as a decoy so his sweetheart could escape. Roscoe might decide he needed a decoy, and obviously he wouldn't choose himself.

"Will, he could use us in ways I don't want to think about." He glanced back at the gold. "There are only two bags to go. We've got to find a way out before he comes for the last one."

"Let's split. I'll search along this side."

In a few minutes, Roscoe appeared at the top again. "Well, well." He laughed. "I see you're still around." His voice turned ugly. "Now, get with it, and tie this rope around another one of those bags."

"What if we don't?" asked Mike.

Roscoe sneered. "You know the answer."

"You're going to leave us here to die anyway."

"Maybe—maybe not."

"I guess you told Joe something like that too," said William.

Roscoe laughed. "Joe was dumb. He knew how to get to this place, but he told me a bunch of stuff about Indian superstitions and wouldn't show me anything." He flashed his light in their faces. "I told him I'd share the gold with him, but he took me on a wild goose chase all over the mountain. Unfortunately, he met with a little accident."

He waved his pistol at them. "Now get busy before you join your friends in spirit as well as in truth."

William climbed over a pile of rocks to stand next to his cousin. "Come on, Mike," he whispered, "don't rile him."

The boys made their way through the rocks and skeletons to a bag. Again, William helped Mike attach the rope, and Roscoe hauled it to the top.

Roscoe beamed his flashlight slowly across the floor of their prison until it came to the one remaining bag. He laughed. "I see we have another. Be back in a moment. Heh heh heh."

Mike knew they didn't have long. He grabbed the torch. "Let's get with it, Will. I'm not about to take the gold away from Mr. Bones over there. This is our last chance."

Carefully stepping among the skeletons and climbing over the rubble, Mike and William investigated every hole and ledge they could find. The torch grew dimmer, and Mike had to strain to see anything.

William grabbed Mike's shoulder and pointed. "Mike, I don't have my glasses and can't tell for sure, but is that what I think it is?" On a level above their heads, a narrow split in the rock seemed to grow wider as it progressed toward the floor above them.

"Let's check it out."

William set the torch in the rubble and cupped his hands. Mike placed a foot in them, and William boosted him to where he could reach the split. He wedged himself in place, and William passed him the torch. Holding it with one hand and bracing himself against the wall, Mike reached down and helped William climb with the other.

They progressed slowly. Again, Mike handed the torch to William and climbed. William passed the torch back and scrambled up behind him. Then they repeated the process all over again.

Finally, Mike reached the top. As he pulled himself onto the surface, the torch faded out completely, and the absolute darkness of the cavern settled in around them.

"Mike!"

"Don't move." Mike felt in his pockets. "You've still got the matches, remember?"

"Oh yeah."

Mike lay next to the split. He listened to William fumbling in his pockets and heard him swear as something fell.

"Will," he called, "you all right?"

"I'll know in a minute. I just dropped all the matches except one."

The match scratched on the rock, and a tiny flame burst into being. He reached down. "Quick, hand it to me. I'll hold it while you climb."

William stretched upward. Mike took the match, but it went out as he grasped William's hand. In the darkness, Mike tugged William up the rest of the way.

"That was close."

William puffed loudly. "Talk about close...look out there."

Across the floor of the cavern, Mike saw the beam from a flashlight moving in their direction. "Get down," he whispered.

They flattened themselves on the cavern floor.

Roscoe moved to the edge of the hole and shone his light into it. "Well, well, heh heh heh. What're we doing? Playing hide-and-seek?" He flashed his light from one wall to another.

Mike watched the beam as Roscoe moved it around the rim. In its glow, Mike saw a column beyond William. Poking him, he nodded toward it. They crawled on their stomachs to the column and hid behind it.

Roscoe moved closer to the edge of the cave-in.

"All right, all right," he called. "Enough of this foolishness. Just one more bag and I'll pull you out of there. Then we can all go home." He flashed his beam of light along the edge of the hole and added, "Or is it possible you've already found a way out?"

As the beam of light approached the column where Mike and William were hiding, it stopped and was directed into the narrow split they had used for their escape.

Mike and William froze, afraid to move or make a sound.

"Maybe I should climb down and get the last bag myself," muttered Roscoe.

Mike looked at the faint shadow of the column created by Roscoe's flashlight. He watched it a moment. It didn't move. Why would Roscoe set the light down and disappear? Maybe he tied off one end of the rope somehow and dropped the other into the hole. Yet, there were no sounds of movement.

If Roscoe could be persuaded to climb down for the last bag of gold, they could untie the rope and leave him for the wolves, the shaman, or the sheriff. It didn't matter.

Mike knew it was risky, but his curiosity was getting the best of him. Edging around the side of the column, he peered at the light lying next to the edge of the hole. Roscoe was nowhere in sight.

Suddenly, a hand clamped down on his shoulder and rudely shoved him forward. "So there you are. Heh heh heh. You don't want to leave a job unfinished, do you?"

CHAPTER 18

Exit

Roscoe picked up the rope and waved one end of it in front of them. "Well, who will it be? Who's going down for the last bag?"

Mike opened his mouth, but before he could argue, Roscoe handed the rope to William. "You. Tie this around your waist. Heh-heh-heh. Your friend will keep me company as a backup."

William slowly pulled the rope around his waist. Before he could tie it, a movement echoed from above, and Roscoe flashed his light up to a ledge near the ceiling of the cavern.

A large, white wolf stared down at them. The animal lifted his head and a piercing howl echoed throughout the chamber.

Mike's heart stood still, and every muscle in his body stiffened. The sound echoed from every direction as William dropped the rope, his eyes wide and his mouth open.

The shaman appeared next to the wolf and held a torch high above his head. "Who dares enter the Guardian's Lair?"

Roscoe responded with his ugly laugh. "Heh heh heh. Dares? Heh heh heh. Sorry to bother your little game, but I figure I can make better use of these bags than you can."

"The gold is cursed," replied the shaman. "It shall remain."

"Oh, and who's going to stop me from taking it? You?"

"Those who enter these chambers can never leave."

Roscoe jerked the pistol from his belt. "Oh, yeah, that's what you think."

He fired, but the shaman and the wolf disappeared as if they were projected images on the wall. The sound of the pistol bounced from wall to wall like a marble in a pinball machine. When it faded, a spooky quiet filled the cave. It made Mike think of the stillness of the wind before a mighty storm.

For a moment, Roscoe held his light on the place where the shaman and wolf disappeared. With a look of confusion, he stuck the pistol under his belt. He turned toward William, but before he could say anything, a low rumble came from deep within the mountain, and the ground vibrated as if a train were approaching on a nearby track.

"Earthquake!" Mike exclaimed. He jerked William down beside him while Roscoe stared about with a stunned look on his face.

"That shot must've started something," said William.

"Yeah, or the shaman did," said Mike. "C'mon." He crawled back toward the base of the column.

Roscoe turned toward them. "Hey! Where do you think you're going?" He reached to pick up the rope, but before he could grasp it, a heavy tremor shook the ground. Dropping the light, he fell to his knees as cracks appeared on the floor of the cavern. Suddenly, with a mighty roar, the ground gave way, and Roscoe screamed in terror as he and a mass of rock tumbled downward on top of the skeletons in the cavern below.

The flashlight still lay near the edge of the hole. Without taking time to think, Mike crawled out to it and yelled, "Roscoe!"

The ground shook again. Mike snatched the light and leaped back. A column crumbled near the hole, and a shower of rubble fell from the ceiling and tumbled into the hole as other parts of the floor broke off and fell.

"Let's get out of here!"

"Which way?" yelled William, choking in a cloud of dust.

Mike pointed with the light. "There... I think."

Bending low, the two of them dashed from one formation to another, grabbing boulders as they went to keep their balance. Mike flashed his light toward an area where the walls narrowed into a passage. "Over there." He tugged on William's arm.

They scrambled into the passage. Nearby, a stalactite crashed, shattering on the ground like a fallen chandelier. A cloud of dust mushroomed behind them as they climbed over a pile of rubble into another cavern.

Mike beamed his flashlight on the walls. "Will, the pictures…" He swung his light to the painting of the large wolf. Its eyes seemed to stare at him as if in anger, and for an instant, Mike froze as if in a trance.

"I was here. I know this place," said William. "Go on, keep moving."

Mike and William ran close to the wall to avoid the sinkhole in the center of the cavern. Near the other side, they ducked low and trotted through the narrow tunnel to the waterfall.

Mike pointed with the light. "Over there. Come on."

The roar of the falls seemed louder than before. Debris from broken stalactites and columns seemed to block their way as Mike ran along the path with William close behind.

Suddenly, Mike stopped, and William plowed into the back of him.

"What?" asked William. "What's wrong?"

Mike shone his light at a wall of boulders and rock. "Wrong? Look!"

"What?"

"You idiot, that's the way out!" More quietly, Mike added, "I guess we ought to say it was the way out."

"We're…we're trapped," whispered William as if it were an unbelievable revelation.

Mike swept the light along the top of the pile and the sides. He moved along the wall. "There's got to be a way. If not here, somewhere." He studied the ceiling, hoping he might find a crack.

The rumbling beneath his feet stopped, and all became still with only the roar of the waterfall dominating the sound around them. Mike sat on a rock, and William flopped down beside him.

For a moment, neither of them said anything. Then softly, William asked, "You think anybody will wonder where we are?"

Mike turned his light on him. "I reckon."

"Do you think they'll look for us?"

"Of course," said Mike. With a sinking feeling, he added, "The trouble is, I'm not sure they'll look in the right place."

"Didn't you tell anybody where you were going?"

"How could I?" Mike sighed. "I left before the folks got back. Besides, I was in a hurry." He added cheerfully, "Still, Karana knows where we are." He turned out the light to save on the batteries and kept talking. He explained about the storm and Karana and talked about outrunning the wolves. He flashed the light on his leg to show William what had happened to his trousers.

William shared how he had come across Roscoe in the bunkhouse. The librarian found the map to the Circle of Fire and forced William into going with him to help drag out the gold.

Mike tried to listen. Nevertheless, while his cousin muttered something about how upset his aunt would be, he drifted into a deep sleep.

***

Later, Mike awoke to the steady roar of the waterfall. He felt the flashlight by his side and turned it on. William lay nearby sound asleep.

Mike shook him. "Will, c'mon. We've got to find a way out."

William blinked his eyes in the glow from the light. "What time is it?"

Flashing the light on his watch, Mike held it to his ear and shook it. "Don't know, but then I don't reckon it makes much difference."

William stretched and rubbed his eyes, then his stomach. "I feel like I haven't eaten in days."

"Yeah, I'm hungry, too, but we've got water." Mike hopped to his feet and added, "C'mon, let's go down and get a drink of breakfast." He led the way back along the trail and wondered if all the shaking had caused any new cracks. Suddenly, he heard a splash and turned his light on William who stood in water, ankle deep.

Mike swung his light toward the lake and gasped as he realized how high the water had risen. He flashed the light on the falls. The water seemed to be pouring out even faster than it had been before.

William stepped back above the path. "What's happening?"

"Somehow, the earthquake's made the water flow faster. The place is filling up." Mike examined a narrow ledge with his light. It passed near an opening just above the water. "Look! There's a hole."

"That ledge isn't very wide," complained William.

"Yeah," agreed Mike, "But it might lead to a way out."

"Wonder where."

"Most any place would be better than where we are now."

Mike climbed up to the ledge and began sliding along against the wall. He stopped and swung the light toward William.

. "I'm ready," said William. He hopped up behind him, grabbed Mike's belt with one hand, and flattened himself against the rock

Mike continued inching his way forward. He reached the hole and made William release his belt so he could climb inside.

Climbing back out, he shook his head. "It's a dead end, but..."

William interrupted. "Listen."

"To what—the waterfall?"

"No." William crouched on the rock. "Aim your light this way. The water's gurgling—you know—like it's going down."

Suddenly the ledge crumbled without warning, and William yelled as he tumbled into the water. Mike grabbed for him but missed, throwing himself off balance and following his cousin into the wet, swirling darkness. The cold water took Mike's breath away as he fought to the surface.

He screamed, "Will!"

A mouthful of water caused Mike to choke as restless currents pulled him back below the surface. The darkness made it impossible to see anything, though his eyes were open. His sense of direction became confused. Holding his breath, he swam with all the strength he could, hoping his struggles would take him upward.

Just as his lungs were about to burst, he broke the surface and gulped a mouthful of air. He had no idea where he came out of the water, but he could feel the current pulling him down again.

Splashing and gasping, he sank into the inky depths. The rocks passed beneath him, and he slid forward as if being sucked into a giant drain. He clawed at the sides of the tunnel, trying to stop his downward plunge, but the swiftness of the current was too strong. After tumbling head over heels, his feet moved forward. He threw his arms over his head for protection as he smashed from side to side. The angle of descent increased as his body shot toward the bowels of the earth. Abruptly, the angle changed upward, and he blasted out into a bright, heavenly light.

CHAPTER 19

Home Again

"Mike."

Someone was calling his name.

"Mike."

He tried to move, but he ached all over. He remembered the bright light. Did that mean he had made it to heaven? If so, why did he feel so sore? He groaned.

Something cool and damp touched his head.

"Mike," insisted a voice. "Mike, are you all right?"

That's a silly question, he thought. Of course, he wasn't all right. If he was, he'd be down on earth instead of up in heaven—or should it be up on earth. Wait! That didn't make sense. He opened his eyes and squinted in the sunlight.

"He's awake," announced the voice.

Mike glanced around. He lay on the grass near the bank of a swift, flowing stream. A pair of shadows moved nearby. He raised his head as the nearest one came into focus. "Dad!"

His father gently pushed him back down, his head dropping back onto a rolled-up jacket. "Hey, lie still. It seems you've had quite an experience."

"Where am I? Where's Mom?"

"You're on Lookout Mountain," said his father. "Your mother and Granddad are on the way to the hospital with William. You're all right, Mike. You're going to be fine."

Mike shielded his eyes. "What about Will?"

"We think he's got a broken collarbone and a concussion. He doesn't remember much. Otherwise, you're just like him—all banged up."

A tall shadow passed in front of him, and Mike glanced up at Karana.

"You are well?" asked the Indian. Mike could see the concern in her eyes.

"Yeah, sort of," said Mike.

Karana nodded.

Mike gazed around. "Where on the mountain are we?"

His dad motioned toward the slope across the stream. "Your grandfather calls it *Indian Writings* because of the cave up there."

Mike grinned. Of course, this was the valley where it all began. Above him, the water spurted out of an opening in the cliff. He shuddered as he looked down stream at the boulder where he and William had met the family of skunks. "Dad, how'd you find us? I know you said not to climb on Lookout Mountain, but there's a reason."

"We'll discuss that later," interrupted his father. "Karana contacted us. She said Roscoe Sweeney had taken William into a cave to look for Indian artifacts. You followed to bring him back."

Mr. Watkins frowned as he continued. "Mike, I know you went for a purpose, but these grounds are private property. They belong to the Apache. Roscoe had no business here, and neither had the two of you. By the way, where is Roscoe?"

"He's gone," said Mike, his eyes widening as he remembered everything that had happened. "We were in the cave, I saw him fall. The whole ceiling fell in on us. He's under tons of rock. Will and I fell into the water, and that's all I remember."

Speechless, Mr. Watkins stared at him a moment, gathered him in his arms, and gave him a hug. "Thank God you're all right. I'd say the two of you are about the luckiest guys alive." He got to his feet, holding Mike like a scoop on the front end of a bulldozer. "I'll get with the sheriff about Roscoe. For now, it's time to join everybody else at the hospital."

Mike felt kind of embarrassed to be carried about like a baby. But he was sore and wasn't sure he could do all the climbing anyway. He hated not being completely open with his father about all that happened, but he knew if any hint got out about there being gold involved, the Lookout grounds of the Apache would be overrun by greedy fortune hunters. He had made a promise, and he intended to keep it. As they were leaving the valley, he looked over his father's shoulder at Karana.

The tall, beautiful Indian responded by raising a hand in farewell. However, before she disappeared into the woods, she did something he had thought impossible.

She smiled.

Mike waved his hand. He didn't really know where most of the coins were anyway. It was all buried somewhere in the rubble. Then with a gasp, he thought about William. He might remember everything and say something he shouldn't.

"Hey, are you all right?" asked his father in a concerned voice.

"Oh, I'm fine, but, Dad, let's hurry to the hospital. I need to talk to Will."

After they passed the rocks where the Spaniard was hidden, Mike's dad set him down, and Mike found he could walk, though stiffly. At the truck, he heard a distant howl. He paused and gazed back at the mountain. A white wolf appeared on a ledge near one end of the valley. Mike shuddered and gasped in pain as strained muscles complained of the sudden movements. He still wasn't sure if the Guardian existed as a real animal or as a phantom.

He gritted his teeth from the soreness of his bruised muscles and crawled into the front seat of the pickup. "Dad, it's sure great to be out of that cave, and we've got to check on Will. But there's a drive-through near the hospital, and I'm about to starve. Let's grab something to eat on the way."

At the hospital, Mike got a few minutes alone with his cousin. A bandage covered William's head and arm. Mike hopped up on the bed. "Hey, are you all right?"

"Other than all my senses being pulverized by an immense steam roller, I couldn't be better."

Mike grinned. "You sound like you're all right."

William shoved his glasses up and stared. "Oh, wow! If you think I look bad, you haven't seen yourself lately. But at least things are a lot clearer than they were. Your mom dug out my spare set of specs—even if they don't fit right."

"You know," said Mike, "it's too bad you never got a clear look at all the gold we left."

"We might still do something about that."

Mike sat on the bed. "Then you do remember everything."

"I had a little trouble at first, but it's all coming back."

Mike sat on the edge of William's bed. "You know we'd never be able to find those coins again. And we really can't tell anyone about it either."

With a groan, William pulled himself into a sitting position. "Why?"

"First of all, we don't have any idea where Roscoe dropped the bags he took. They're probably buried under tons of rock. There's no way we could get to them."

William flopped back on his pillow. "Yeah, you're probably right. It's unfortunate, though. I can conjure all sorts of things I could do with a bag of gold coins."

"There's something else."

"What?"

"If we tell what we found, all sorts of people would climb up on the mountain with air hammers and stuff. You know how greedy folks get when they think there's gold around."

"You mean, like Roscoe?"

"Exactly, and if that happened, the Circle of Fire would be trampled over and dug up. I promised Karana to keep their secret. It's about the only way I know of that we can pay her back for help-ing us."

William nodded his head. "Yeah, I guess you're right."

"As far as anyone else is concerned," continued Mike, "Roscoe took you up there looking for arrowheads and old Indian stuff, and

I followed. The cave collapsed, Roscoe got caught in it, and we got away."

Mike's dad entered the room. "Come on, Mike. The doctor wants to check you over."

Mike nodded at William and made a face. "See you later."

As Mike left the room, William called after him, "Watch out for the medic with the bandages. You'll come out looking like a mummified humanoid."

Mike shook his head and muttered, "At least, I'd still be talking like a human."

***

At almost noon the next day, Mike awoke. Painfully, he pushed himself into a sitting position. The past day's experience seemed like a dream except for all the bruises. William slept nearby; his head wrapped in bandages, and his arm strapped tight against his body.

Mike propped himself up on one elbow. "Will?"

William groaned a little and turned on his side.

"Will, you awake?"

"Of course, I'm awake," William replied gruffly. He glanced wildly about the room. "What's happening?"

Mike grinned. "We're home, dodo. Remember?"

William sat up, moaned a little, and lay back down.

"I'm about to starve," said Mike. "You know, I bet we could make a little trip to the kitchen, and none would be the wiser."

William sat up again, put on his glasses, and dropped his feet to the floor. "I'm with you. Let's go."

The kitchen was unoccupied. Mike got some peanut butter out of the cabinet while William went for the bread. After filling their stomachs, they headed back to their room.

"You know, I just thought of something." William stretched out on his bed.

"What?"

"Remember when we were looking through the book in the library—you know—the one about unsolved robberies?"

"Yeah?" Mike raised an eyebrow.

"There was one anecdote in it about a robbery over in Taos that happened just a few years after the one at Springer."

"So?" Mike dropped his feet over the edge of his bed.

"Well, it seems some old miner brought a bag of gold into Taos for weighing. A French trapper murdered him, took the bag, and then disappeared back into the mountains never to be seen again."

"Uh huh." Mike picked up a pillow and started fluffing it in his lap.

"So I was thinking. Taos isn't far. There might be a whole mine full of gold nuggets somewhere just waiting to be found."

Mike said nothing and continued to concentrate on his pillow.

"I mean, we might hike into those mountains near Taos and explore the mines up there. Who knows what we might find?"

Mike held his pillow up in front of him and studied it as if he were looking at a piece of art.

"Well, what do you think?"

"Will, open your mouth."

"Why?"

"I want to see how narrow I've got to make this pillow for it to fit."

William grabbed his pillow and held it in front of him. "Now wait. You wouldn't attack a one-armed man wearing glasses."

"Who said I needed two arms to take care of you?"

As Mike drew back his pillow, William sat up and swung his pillow into the side of Mike's head, knocking him off balance.

"Ooooh, that means war!"

And the battle began.

ABOUT THE AUTHOR

A former educator, Carl Watson taught Language Art classes in both elementary and junior high schools. As a published author, his works appeared in both adults' and children's magazines. He is a graduate of North Texas State University and Texas Wesleyan University (ME). He assisted in writing a syllabus for Social Studies in the Fort Worth Public School System. The Fort Worth National Bank awarded him a fellowship to continue his studies in creative writing. His work has appeared in several children's magazines and in stories for the Methodist Publishing House, Child Life, and in True West Magazine.

Watson's first novel, *Kid Clay*, is a historical, western, adventure story for middle grade students based on his grandfather's experience as a teen cowboy. It was awarded Texas Author's First Place in YA historical fiction in 2018. His second novel, *Silent Journey*, is about the difficulties and challenges of a deaf boy and his dog.

CPSIA information can be obtained
at www.ICGtesting.com
Printed in the USA
BVHW070626151222
654214BV00005B/507